"I worshiped you, Cole!"

she threw at him, half hurt, half angry.

His jaw went taut. "When will you understand that I don't want hero worship from you?" he shot at her.

"What do you want?" she challenged.

He moved toward her before she could read the intent in his glittering eyes.

She shrank back as he propped his lean, brown hands on the wall on either side of her head and eased his body against hers, pinning her there in a silence that burned with emotion.

"Let me show you what I want," he growled, and what she read in his eyes made her pulse run wild with anticipation.

Available From Diana Palmer

HEATHER'S SONG

Heather Shaw had loved Cole Everett for years, though the sentiment had never been returned. But when Cole got a look at a *very* grown-up Heather, would his feelings of mere fondness turn into full-fledged passion?

FIRE AND ICE

Coldhearted Cal Van Dyne thought he was immune to romance—until he met Margie Silver, whose business was happy endings. Now Cal's icy demeanor was in danger of thawing under this warm woman's passionate fire!

THE AUSTRALIAN

Australian rancher John Sterling had always been intrigued by the girl-next-door, Priscilla Johnson. He was determined to have Priscilla at any cost, but was John willing to pay if the price was his heart . . . ?

HEATHER'S SONG

DIANA PALMER

Silhouette® Books

Published by Silhouette Books New York

SILHOUETTE BOOKS
300 East 42nd St., New York, N.Y. 10017

HEATHER'S SONG

Copyright © 1982 by Diana Palmer

All rights reserved. Except for use in any review, the reproduction or utilization of this work in whole or in part in any form by any electronic, mechanical or other means, now known or hereafter invented, including xerography, photocopying and recording, or in any information storage or retrieval system, is forbidden without the permission of the publisher, Silhouette Books, 300 E. 42nd St., New York, N.Y. 10017

ISBN: 0-373-48267-1

Published Silhouette Books 1982, 1988, 1993

All the characters in this book have no existence outside the imagination of the author and have no relation whatsoever to anyone bearing the same name or names. They are not even distantly inspired by any individual known or unknown to the author, and all incidents are pure invention.

® and ™: Trademarks used with authorization. Trademarks indicated with ® are registered in the United States Patent and Trademark Office, the Canada Trade Mark Office and in other countries.

Printed in the U.S.A.

Available From Diana Palmer

Chapter One

The willowy blond was spotlighted in the center of the stage, her long platinum hair gleaming, her soft blue eyes half-closed and faintly sultry as she sang. Her voice, as clear and soulful as a bell in late evening, held the audience spellbound.

Heather Shaw was only twenty, but she had the stage presence of a much older performer. This was her first big break, though by no means her first performance. Tonight was the culmination of two years' work, the moment she had looked forward to ever since she'd set out to win her independence from Cole.

As the last notes of her finale were followed by loud, enthusiastic applause, she felt strangely empty. She stood there, a vision in black lace and silver, and wondered if this was all there was to success.

When she'd left the ranch, Cole had warned her that success wasn't the gleaming treasure she imagined. "It won't be enough," he'd said in that cool, controlled voice of his. "You'll miss Big Spur."

Heather sighed as she took off her stage makeup, changed into street clothes, and got her jacket and purse. It was well past midnight, and she wanted nothing more than her bed. Cole was right—she did miss Big Spur.

She climbed into her little sports car with a wry smile. Maybe it *would* be best if she gave up her ambition and went home to the ranch. The rain was misting all around her, and she shivered, uncertain whether it was the cold or a sudden wave of homesickness that had caused her to tremble.

She pulled out into the sparse traffic and sat impatiently at a red light. Staring through the rain-blurred windshield at the nearly empty road, she wondered what Cole would say if he could see the loneliness in her eyes now.

The light changed and she stepped on the accelerator, in a hurry to get home to her warm apartment. She sped down the narrow street, unable to see the car coming at her on the wrong side of the road until she rounded a curve. And then it was too late. She gasped, hit the wheel too hard, and heard with a sense of unreality the screeching of tires, the crushing of metal, the wild shattering of broken glass....

* * *

Heather woke to darkness. It lurked outside the drawn blinds on the window, and she felt alone and afraid. Her slender body moved anxiously between the crispness of clean cotton sheets in the narrow hospital bed. She wanted to scream, but that was impossible. Her long, pink-tipped fingers went to her throat in frustration, and tears washed her pale blue eyes. If only Cole would come!

Her eyes darted again to the blinds and she frowned, tossing her long platinum hair restlessly on the pillow, teasing it into curling wisps. Surely he would have come as soon as he heard about the accident! Despite their disagreements, the stepbrother she worshiped would never have deserted her at a time like this. Cole could be cruel, but he was never heartless.

She shivered under the thin sheet. The heat was on, of course, but the room was still chilly. She'd have given a lot for one of the quilts her stepmother Emma liked to make on cold winter nights.

The door opened, and a smiling young nurse came in with a tray. "Time for your dinner," she said pleasantly. She put the tray down and paused to rearrange the bedclothes before moving the food within reach.

Heather tried to speak, but it wasn't any different now than it had been last night when they'd extricated her from the wreckage of the sports car. No sound came from her throat except a hoarse croak. The fear showed in every line of her delicate face and in the pale blue Siamese cat eyes under the tousled platinum hair that fell in untidy wisps around her shoulders.

The nurse glanced down and read her expression. "It's not permanent," she assured her. "Just a result of shock from the accident. You'll talk again, dear."

But I'm a professional singer, she wanted to protest. I'm a singer, and I've just gotten my first big break! Why did this have to happen to me now? I'm committed to a two-week run at the Bon Soir, and now everything's ruined!

Her eyes closed on a wave of nausea. If only it hadn't been raining. If only she'd listened to Cole and bought a bigger car, one that wouldn't have gone into a skid on the wet road.... Heather's soft eyes filled with tears. She glanced around at the bedside table and mimed her frustration at having nothing to write with.

"I'll get you something," the nurse promised. "Back in a minute."

Picking at the food in front of her, Heather watched the nurse's retreating figure. She felt so lost and alone. Even Gil Austin hadn't shown up yet. He was her best friend in Houston, a reporter who'd been doing a feature story on the band she was appearing with when she met him. Gil was a live wire, and he'd taken the shy young singer under his wing, watching over her almost as protectively as Cole. Gil and Cole were even about the same age, Gil thirty, Cole thirty-three. But the resemblance ended there. Gil had fair hair and green eyes, and was always smiling. Cole's hair was dark, his eyes were gray, and his face resembled deeply tanned stone. His life was the enormous ranch he and

Heather's father had built up together. Big Spur was a showplace, and Cole never tired of it. No woman had ever been able to nudge it to one side long enough to get him to make a commitment. Cole didn't like ties of any kind.

"There you are!" came a breathless, relieved voice from the doorway.

Gil Austin let the door slide shut again as he came forward, his eyes worried, his fair hair tousled, his habitual smile noticeably missing as he studied the slender young form under the sheets. "Johnson sent me to Miami on a story." He grimaced, looking wounded. "If I hadn't been out of town, I'd have known about the accident long before now. I'm sorry, little girl!"

She tried to speak, but the effort was futile. She nodded instead.

He caught her small hand and squeezed it. "Are you hurt bad?"

She shook her head, pointing at her throat, and smiled again.

The nurse came back in with a pad and pen and handed it to Heather, smiling pleasantly at Gil. "Are you her stepbrother?"

Gil shook his head, frowning. "Hasn't he been notified?"

"Of course." The nurse nodded. "His name and phone number were in her purse. The attending physician called him from the emergency room. That," she added with a hasty glance at Heather, "was very early this morning."

Gil, too, looked at Heather, who was busily scribbling a note on the pad. "Taking his time, isn't he?" he asked quietly.

The nurse nodded with a sigh. "If you're through with your dinner, I'll take it away now. Ring if you need anything." She smiled at Heather.

Heather smiled back and handed Gil a note explaining how the accident happened and asking if he'd make sure they had notified Cole. "He'd be here if he knew," she'd written.

Gil frowned at the faith in her bright eyes. He knew how she worshiped Cole Everett. But he also knew how fiery their relationship was, and how much Cole disapproved of his stepsister's singing career. He wasn't convinced that Everett might not be teaching her a painful lesson by his absence. The Texas rancher had a reputation for being difficult and temperamental. Gil, who covered the entertainment beat for the paper, had never met him, but he'd heard the business reporters talk about him and shudder. Everett was a millionaire several times over, and something of a power in Texas politics. A man with that kind of wealth would naturally be arrogant, but they said Everett made an art of it.

"I'll go and check now, okay?" he asked, forcing a smile he didn't feel. She looked so helpless lying there, so vulnerable. He wanted to protect her, but despite the weeks they'd been dating, she wouldn't let him get close to her. He wondered if anyone had ever been able to measure up to Everett in her eyes. Her awe of the man was almost unnatural.

He left her long enough to check with the head nurse, and was informed in no uncertain terms that Mr. Everett had indeed been advised of his stepsister's condition. The woman didn't know why he hadn't come, but she promised to have someone call him a second time.

Gil stayed with Heather until visiting hours ended, when he told her he'd have to go. She clung to his hand, but only for an instant. He left with promises to return early in the morning, and she held back her tears until the door closed behind him.

Being alone was frightening. It was all too easy to lie there and brood about the loss of her voice. She'd talk again, they said. This was just a temporary condition, hysterical paralysis of the larynx, the doctor had told her. When she got over the shock of the accident her voice would return. But could she sing again? She bit her lower lip. Oh, Cole, if only Cole were here, she wouldn't be afraid . . . !

The sound of a cold, angry voice penetrated her depression. She blinked her eyes, straightening in the bed. She half turned toward the door, where the voice was coming from.

"I don't want excuses!" it growled. "I want to know why in hell I wasn't notified!"

Cole! She sat erect, the sheet falling away from the shapeless green hospital gown they'd put her in, and stared at the door with her heart in her soft eyes. There was a placating murmur just before the door was thrown open and her stepbrother walked in.

His hard, dark face was like a thunderhead, his silvery eyes blazing under his jutting brow. Tall, dark, blatantly masculine, he towered over the small, nervous nurse behind him. Heather's pale eyes brightened with tears at the sight of him, so arrogantly commanding. All the arguments between them were abruptly forgotten, and she held out her arms like a hurt child seeking comfort.

His silvery eyes flashed at the gesture, and for an instant he looked as if he wanted to throw something. He tossed his cream-colored Stetson into a chair and bent to lift her slender body into his hard arms, cradling her against his broad chest as he eased down beside her on the bed.

She wept brokenly, her tears staining the brown fabric of his vested suit, and he held her even closer.

"I didn't know," he ground out, his deep voice rough with emotion. "I'd have been here hours ago if anyone had bothered to notify me."

"Mr. Everett, you were called," the nurse protested gently. "Honestly, you were. The attending physician put the call through while I was in the emergency room; I heard him give the message."

Cole glared at her, his eyes dangerous with anger. "No one spoke to *me,*" he said deliberately.

The nurse swallowed. "That's possible, of course. We're very sorry about the mix-up." She slipped out quietly, closing the door gently behind her.

Cole drew back to look down at Heather's wet face. His eyes narrowed when he studied her wan cheeks in their frame of curling platinum hair. She looked like a whipped child. "Was it bad?" he asked softly.

She shook her head and tried to smile. Her eyes openly worshiped him. Cole was the biggest thing in her young life. She might fight with him, rebel against his arrogance, his absolute domination, but she loved him obsessively and she made no secret of it. It had been that way from the very beginning, when she was thirteen and Emma and Cole came to live at Big Spur.

His eyes slid down over her body in the hospital gown, lingering on a bruise at her collarbone. He reached down and touched it, and she stiffened instinctively at the unfamiliar sensation. "You're bruised," he said harshly, tracing the purplish area angrily. "I warned you about that damned little car."

Her lower lip pouted at him and her eyes flashed. She wanted so badly to speak, to argue, but all she could do was fume.

He looked down at her steadily. There was no expression on his impassive face, but for an instant something gleamed in his eyes.

"Have they sent anyone for your clothes?" he asked.

She shook her head, reaching for the pad and pen. "Hasn't been time," she wrote.

"I'll bring your things," he said. He stood up, flexing his shoulders as if he hadn't had much rest. Probably he hadn't had any, she thought, studying him. Cole went like a dynamo, all the time. Her gaze was caught by the attractive brown western-cut suit he was wearing. She couldn't help noticing the way it emphasized his broad shoulders and narrow waist and hips, the way it clung to his powerful thighs like a second skin. There was something so sensuous about Cole, about the way he moved....

She squashed the disquieting thought. "Home?" she mouthed.

One dark eyebrow went up. "Your apartment or the ranch?" he asked.

She stared down at her fingers and her mouth pouted. "The ranch," she scribbled, hating her own weakness.

"It won't be that bad," he promised. "Emma could use the company. I've been away a lot."

"Not with cattle," she wrote on the pad, flashing him a knowing look. "Not in winter."

A rare smile touched his hard, chiseled mouth for a second, and she caught herself wondering if he ever used that smile on other women. It was devastating.

She shifted slightly in the bed, trying to ease the ache that seemed to affect her whole body. He leaned down and his long, brown fingers touched the white bandage that covered one of many abrasions on her arm. "Does it hurt, baby?" he asked.

He was the only man who'd ever called her that. It wasn't an endearment she particularly liked, but Cole made it sound special.

She shook her head, reached her own fingers up to cover his, and caressed them lovingly.

The gesture seemed to bother him. He drew back as if she'd burned him and quickly moved away from the bed, ramming both hands into his pockets as he prowled around the small hospital room.

Heather felt rejected. Cole was acting so distant tonight. It was as if he didn't want to be in the same room with her.

He drew a sharp, impatient breath, and when he turned back to her, his firm lips made a thin line. "How can I talk to you like this?" he growled.

She lifted her pad and wrote him a note. "I can write," she scribbled, showing it to him with a smile.

"I know," he said, "but it's not the same. How long will it be before you can talk?"

She shrugged. "They aren't sure," she wrote.

"I'll talk with the doctor," he said, taking over, as usual. He looked so impossibly arrogant that she smiled at him, her whole heart in her adoring eyes.

His own silvery eyes snapped at her. "Don't look at me like that," he said abruptly.

She gaped at him, the confusion plain in her wounded eyes.

He turned away, grabbing up his Stetson. "I'll be back in the morning," he said without facing her. "I'll bring you a gown when I come."

She stared after him in bewilderment. Something must be very wrong for Cole to treat her so coolly. She only wondered what it was.

He was back the next morning, after she'd had her bath and her breakfast, with a small overnight bag that held a gown and some cosmetics.

"You can leave tomorrow," he said curtly, dropping down into the armchair beside her bed. "I've told your doctor we'll let our family physician take charge of your treatment."

She hid a grin behind her hand. She could see Cole having it out with the wiry little doctor on her case.

"I've got to fly down to New Orleans for the day," he continued. "But I'll try to stop by before they put you to bed for the night."

He made her sound like a toddler who needed a teddy bear and a bottle, and she glared at him.

One dark eyebrow went up. "Want to scratch me, kitten?" he asked.

"Yes," she mouthed angrily.

His pale eyes slid down over the sheet that covered her thin young body. "You're not up to my weight," he remarked.

She hit the bed with a clenched fist and he threw back his head and chuckled softly, the sound oddly pleasant in the stillness of the room. As he stood up, she noticed how striking he looked in a gray suit that matched his silver eyes. He fumbled at his shirt pocket for a cigarette and then brought one to his beautifully chiseled mouth.

"Habit," he growled, lighting the cigarette. "I don't even like the taste of them anymore." He leaned down and carelessly brushed her cheek with his firm lips. "Don't give the doctor any trouble while I'm gone," he warned.

"That's your department, not mine," she wrote saucily.

"You little brat," he said, making an endearment of it. "See you tonight."

She beamed at him, but she didn't reach out to touch his hand, as she would have a day earlier. It was becoming increasingly obvious that he didn't want to be touched.

Gil visited her later on, and leered at the picture she made in the pale blue chiffon gown Cole had brought.

"Talk about seductive," he said in a theatrically husky voice. "You look good enough to eat."

"Hospital food will give you indigestion," she scribbled with a grin.

He laughed. "Yes, I suppose it will, but I'm not a patient. Where *did* you get that gown?"

"It's hospital issue," she lied on paper.

"Smart hospital. No patient, male patient, that is, would ever want to escape if all the female patients wore gowns like that." He leaned forward in his chair. "Where's your stepbrother? They told me he came last night. Excuse me, *stormed in* last night," he added with a grin. "At least two of the nurses are being treated for shock, I hear."

"He was mad," she wrote on her pad.

"He should have jumped on whoever forgot to give him the message," Gil pointed out, "not on the poor nurses. They couldn't help it."

She sighed. "The nurses were here," she wrote.

"Oh." He nodded. "And the poor soul who didn't deliver the message wasn't. I wish I knew the devil's name, I'd send flowers in advance."

Heather's face lit up in a smile. Gil was such fun to be around. He made all the shadows go away, and while she was with him she forgot her fears and was able to relax.

He was telling her stories about his early days as a reporter when the door swung open and Cole walked in to find Gil Austin sitting comfortably on the side of Heather's bed. Cole stood quietly in the doorway, and his very stance spelled trouble.

Heather could almost see his neck hair bristling. That silvery glitter in his eyes was dangerous, and she didn't like the way he fixed his icy gaze on the man sitting beside her on the bed.

"The stepbrother, I presume," Gil said with irrepressible good humor as he rose to face the newcomer.

Cole wasn't amused. He glared at the younger man, his powerful body held in rigid control.

Gil cleared his throat, disconcerted by that level stare. "I'm Gil Austin," he said, breaking the silence. "I cover the entertainment beat for the *News Herald*—and Heather's my girl." He glanced possessively at the slender young woman under the white sheets.

Cole's eyes seemed to explode. His jaw went even tauter in his dark face. "A reporter," he said, making an insult of the word. His eyes swept contemptuously over the shorter man before he turned back to Heather. "I'll come by for you first thing in the morning," he told her curtly. "Is there anything you want from your apartment? You'll be at the ranch for a few weeks, at least."

Heather scribbled "my coat." She grimaced at the faint amusement in Cole's eyes. She was superstitious about the ankle-length ermine coat Cole had given her for her eighteenth birthday. She never traveled without it.

"I'll bring it," he promised. "Anything else?"

"My purse," she scribbled, "my old one—in the closet."

He frowned.

"I keep my important papers in it," she wrote, "and my money."

His eyes narrowed. "You won't need a bankroll to come home with."

She sighed with irritation. If only she could talk. She wanted to tell him she didn't need his handouts...but he read the emotion in her eyes and lifted his head in that arrogant way he had. She could have hit him.

"Can I do anything?" Gil asked, feeling left out.

"We can manage," Cole said abruptly, sparing the man a glance.

"I'd like to visit Heather while she's recuperating," he persisted.

Cole turned around and stared right through him. "The last thing she's going to need right now are visitors," he said without even pretending courtesy.

Heather gaped at him. Cole had always been possessive, but now he was acting as though he owned her. Why couldn't she have visitors?

"Heather needs peace and quiet to get over the trauma of the accident. She'll heal quicker with family," Cole added, "and I'm going to take them to Nassau for a week or so, anyway. She can call you when she's back on her feet."

Gil hesitated. It was the first time Heather had known him to be without a comeback.

"Get some rest, baby," Cole told her, bending to brush his hard lips against her hair. "I'll be here early, so don't stay up too late with your boyfriend," he added pointedly. "Good night, Austin," he said, pinning the other man with his narrowed eyes.

Gil cleared his throat. "You're right, she does look tired. Good night, little one," he said, resisting the urge to kiss her before he left. Everett looked frankly dangerous. "Nice to have met you," he added, pausing to smile at Heather. "I'll be in touch."

"Over my dead body," Cole muttered when he'd gone, and Heather noticed that one lean hand had all but crushed the crown of his Stetson.

"Why don't you like him?" she wrote on the pad, holding it up with a frown.

"He's too old for you," he shot right back.

"I like him," she scribbled angrily.

But he didn't even answer her. "Emma's cooking your favorite dishes," he said pleasantly enough. "She ran Mrs. Jones out of the kitchen to start getting everything ready. Mothers!"

She smiled involuntarily. Emma might only be her stepmother, but she was as dear to Heather as if there'd been a blood tie between them. She sighed and closed her eyes. Maybe she did need to be alone for a while. Maybe it would do her good to get away from everyone who might remind her of her career and the strangely unsatisfying life she'd made for herself in Houston.

She opened her eyes suddenly to find Cole watching her. She dropped her gaze quickly to the bedclothes, wondering at the way her pulse was misbehaving.

"Good night, baby," he said curtly and was gone before she could get her pulse under control.

Chapter Two

The flight to Branntville took hardly any time at all, and Heather watched the flat barren landscape with eyes that remembered it in spring, when the bluebonnets were blooming along with the black-eyed Susans and the trees were a hundred different soft shades of green. She smiled at the memory, and Cole took his eyes away from the controls long enough to read the expression on her flushed face.

"And you were willing to give it all up to sing in a nightclub," he scoffed. "Still think it was a good trade—clean air for smoky rooms?"

She tossed her hair impatiently and glared up at him.

A slow, lazy smile touched his chiseled mouth. "All right, Sunflower." He chuckled, using his childhood nickname for her. "I get the message."

She tore her gaze away from his. Cole had a dark charm that must be devastating when he wanted something from a woman, she mused, letting her eyes focus on the beautifully masculine hands at the controls of the twin-engine Cessna. They were long-fingered and dark, and they held the promise of great strength. His mouth, too, was strong, with a sensuality she was only now beginning to notice. The thought brought a slight frown to her face. Would he be a gentle lover? She flushed, vividly remembering the night last year when she saw him kiss Tessa at her birthday party, his mouth rough, not an inch of space between his hard-muscled body and Tessa's.... The sight had been disturbing to Heather, although she didn't know why. She carried the picture in her mind for days afterward: Tessa had been clinging to Cole like ivy, as if his kiss was everything she needed from life. No, she thought uneasily, Cole wouldn't be gentle. He was a man of extremes, and she sensed that his passions were strong ones. He wouldn't be satisfied with the brief, cool kisses she bestowed on Gil Austin.

She shook herself mentally. Her own thoughts were shocking her, so she turned her attention out the window and watched for the familiar white fences that marked the outlying boundaries of Big Spur.

Minutes later, the house came into view below, surrounded by tall pecan and oak trees. It was brick, its architecture reminiscent of an English manor house. A long driveway circled in front of the entrance, lined with dogwoods that bloomed in white profusion each spring and a myriad of flowering shrubs. In her mind's eye, Heather could see the interior of the towering mansion, the main reception rooms all opening off the center hall with its delightful winding staircase and massive crystal chandelier. The interior rooms were spacious, and the den where Cole did his paperwork had a huge stone fireplace and a very striking Belgian area rug done in deep wine. There was a three-car garage, a tennis court, a swimming pool, and a patio with masses of rose bushes. It was like something out of a storybook, or the Old South—which wasn't at all surprising, since the Shaws had emigrated to East Texas from Georgia. Heather's great-grandfather had built the house, back in the days of the great cattle drives, and it had had its share of famous and infamous guests. In fact, Branntville itself was located on the old Chisholm Trail, a fact that had always excited Heather as a child.

The house was technically Emma's now, willed to her by Heather's late father. Heather never begrudged her stepmother that bequeathal. Emma had loved her stepdaughter like her own child, and that love had been returned full measure. It hurt to remember that Heather's own mother had been a rather cool person, all elegance and high fashion and very little emotion.

They were coming down now, Cole's brown hands firm and confident on the controls as he eased the

Cessna onto the family airstrip, nestled in the midst of thousands of acres of prime cattle land. Cole and her father had built the ranch up slowly over the years, investing their initially modest profits in new stock to improve their herd. Now, Cole had one of the finest ranches in Texas, a ranch that was famous for its blooded stock and champion bulls. Heather felt a sense of pride in her stepbrother. He had a keen business head, and he radiated power. He could make or break a politician in this part of the state, and he was an avid conservationist.

The plane touched down lightly on the runway and Cole taxied it to a stop near the silver side of the hangar and cut the engine. "Home," he told her with a flash of pride in his silver eyes.

She smiled at him, the emotion she felt evident in her eyes, in the parting of her soft mouth. His gaze whipped down to her pink lips with a suddenness that was devastating in its effect on her pulse. She almost gasped at the newness of the look, and the surprise was in her eyes when his gaze shot back up to meet hers.

She turned quickly and tried to open the door, fumbling with it nervously.

"Something wrong, honey?" Cole asked in a strange tone. He leaned across her, his hard-muscled arm pressing against her breasts for an instant, his warm breath in her hair as he opened the door.

She scrambled out as if mad dogs were chasing her, and she thought she heard soft, amused laughter behind her as she reached the pavement.

One of the ranch hands had driven down to get them in the station wagon, and Heather was careful to get in the backseat before Cole could herd her into the front with him. Nothing showed on that impassive face, but she had the strangest feeling that he was amused by her. She could still see that unfamiliar look in his eyes, the darkness making them slate gray, the totally adult glitter something she'd never experienced. Cole had never treated her as anything except his younger sister. But there was nothing remotely filial about that look, and she remembered without wanting to that there was no blood relationship to protect her from Cole. Her innocence would be no match for his obvious experience, and if he could upset her like this just by looking at her, Heaven only knew what would happen if he touched her....

That thought sent a burst of wild excitement singing through her slender young body, and her face blushed as dusky as an autumn sunset. She kept her eyes down so that Cole wouldn't notice—even though he was talking business with the ranch hand.

She'd never considered Cole in this light before. It was a little frightening. She'd watched him charm women with a sense of pride, feeling safe because she was his stepsister. She'd always been shielded from his devastating masculinity. But now she'd stepped out from behind that shield, and she was vulnerable for the first time. She felt like a fawn taking its first steps into a meadow, wondering what dangers lay beyond the quiet, dark glade.

She bit her lower lip hard. She wanted to crawl back into her cocoon and forget what she'd been thinking. Cole was far too dangerous for a novice.

They were driving near the river now, and Heather remembered almost drowning there the first summer Cole and Emma lived at Big Spur. Cole had plucked her out of the water, a shivering little thirteen-year-old with big blue eyes. She'd been his possession since that day, and he'd treated her like one. He'd always had a hand in the major decisions of her life. Her parties, her friends, her travels had all been dictated by Cole, even before her father's death. Her education at an exclusive Swiss girls' school—which she'd hated—had been his idea too. But when it came to singing, she'd managed to get her own way. Emma had stood by her, especially after a well-known promoter named Pete Howell had raved about her talent. Her first appearance at a local nightclub had led to several other offers, and engagement after engagement followed until the big break finally came—the two-week engagement, that she'd just been starting the night of the accident.

"...otherwise, it's been going smoothly," the ranch hand was saying. "Bill said to tell you he sure was sorry he didn't get word to you about Miss Shaw. He got busy...."

"Which is no damned excuse at all," Cole shot back, his silver eyes blazing. "By God, I'll tear a strip off him for that!"

His hard, chiseled mouth made a thin line, and Heather was glad she couldn't see his eyes from the backseat. There was a white-hot anger in his otherwise controlled voice. But then, everything about Cole was controlled. Mr. Cool, she used to call him behind his back. No matter how she tried, she never could rattle him. Her worst tempers only amused him. She'd worn herself out against the rock of his will without accomplishing anything. Her young adulthood had been full of rages. And Cole took them in stride, either ignoring her antics or putting an end to them with a well-placed look and a firm command. She'd never stood up to him until she wanted a career enough to throw caution to the winds. But without Emma's careful pleading, she'd never have won. She'd never seen anyone match Cole. And she never expected to. She felt sorry for Bill, whoever he was. Cole could be utterly cruel.

They wound up the long driveway with its rows of dogwoods, bare now in the winter chill. The house was austerely elegant amid the dark skeletons of the huge oak and pecan trees. No sooner had the station wagon pulled up at the front steps than Emma Everett Shaw came running down them like a silver-haired whirlwind, her deep brown eyes shimmering with excitement, her arms opened wide in welcome.

Heather ran into those slender, outstretched arms like a baby rabbit into its hutch, the pitiful croak of a sob tearing out of her throat.

"My baby," Emma cooed, nestling the tumble of waving platinum hair against her shoulder. "My poor baby, you're safe now, you're home, Emma's here."

That made her cry even more. How many times in her tragedy-torn young life had those words been whispered at her ear? How many tears had poured onto Emma's thin shoulders? The older woman smelled of spices and flour instead of the expensive perfume she connected with her late mother.

Emma was unpretentious, taking her wealth and position for granted. She could charm beggars and kings alike, and Heather had seen her hide a twenty-dollar bill in a farm woman's pocket when there was a money problem in the family that Emma knew about. She delighted in being sneaky about her contributions. No one knew exactly how much money she donated to charity, or in what incredible ways she went about her good works. Heather had known her to anonymously pay a monstrous hospital bill that some down-on-his-luck new father couldn't manage without insurance, and then pretend to be surprised when some member of her garden club told her about it.

Heather cried even harder. Disloyal though it seemed to admit it, her own mother had never cared so much. And Heather loved Emma in a way she could never have loved the fragile, cold piece of porcelain her mother had been.

"That's enough," Cole said suddenly. He separated the two women and, holding Heather roughly by the arm, herded her up the stairs. "I don't mind a few tears, but you can't have hysterics on the front steps."

Her bright, flaming eyes glared up at him violently, and she wanted to hit him. Behind them, Emma was moving quickly up the steps, muttering under her breath. Heather almost smiled. All her life, Emma had muttered at men—first at her husband, then at Heather's father, and now at Cole. It was her own form of passive rebellion, and Heather couldn't help being amused by it. Emma muttered with style.

Once they were in the house, Emma smiled gently at the tear-stained face of her stepdaughter. "Go upstairs and rest, sweetheart," she said softly, "and I'll bring you some hot chocolate. Would you like that?"

Heather's blue eyes lit up. Hot chocolate had always soothed her; it was Emma's answer to chicken soup. She nodded enthusiastically, pausing to throw a hostile glance in Cole's general direction before she held on to the curved, polished wood of the bannister and moved slowly up the beige carpeted staircase to her old room.

She threw open the door and let her tired eyes drink in the sight of the delightfully pink room. The wallpaper was pale pink and matched the thick quilted coverlet and pillow shams on the double bed. There was a full-length mirror on the closet door, and a crystal lamp on the antique washstand against the wall. The carpeting was the same soft beige as in the rest of the house, and there was a wing chair upholstered in fabric that matched the wallpaper.

Heather settled herself on the window seat and looked out over the white-fenced ranch, ignoring Cole as he entered the room to place her bags on the floor before coming to stand beside her.

He followed her gaze to the sweep of land in its winter desolation. The red-coated cattle were massed at feed troughs where silage was taking the place of lush green grass in their diets. Paddocks near the barn sported handsome Appaloosa stallions and two white-coated fillies in separate pastures. Heather sighed, remembering what it was like to ride a horse out through the fields, to hear the lazy creak of saddle leather and to feel the spring breeze wafting in her loosened hair.

"When you're a little stronger, I'll take you riding," Cole said suddenly, as if he'd looked into her mind. It was an uncanny habit he'd always had, one that never failed to stun her. "That is, if you haven't forgotten how to ride."

She glared at him, meeting the challenge in his polished silver eyes as she jerked her head deliberately from side to side.

A mocking smile touched his chiseled mouth. "I can almost see the words in your mind," he mused, making her feel more child than woman.

She hit out at him unexpectedly. It was the only alternative to the scalding tirade she couldn't produce—but it proved equally ineffective. He caught her wrist with his lean, powerful fingers and jerked her against him. His other hand tangled in the long, silken ribbon of her hair, subduing her effortlessly as he pulled her head back until her stunned eyes met his.

"Don't tempt me," he said quietly, his darkening gaze sweeping across her flushed face, taking in the creamy skin, the fullness of her mouth. "You're not too big to spank, Sunflower."

She struggled, but he only held her closer, mocking her with his lean, surprising strength. He'd never held her like this before, and she'd never fought with him physically. It was new, heady, to tempt Cole into violence.

She pushed against him and he ended the unequal struggle all too easily, jerking her ruthlessly closer against his hard body. His face was so close that she could feel his warm, smoky breath on her forehead.

"Still fighting me?" he growled. "When are you going to learn that if there's any bending to be done between us, you'll do it?"

She subsided against him, her eyes blazing, wide with fury. "I hate you!" she mouthed deliberately.

He chuckled softly. "No, you don't," he said, his glittering eyes narrow with amusement as he looked down at her. "You hate not being able to argue with me, but you don't hate me. I'll never let that happen, Heather."

The shock of hearing her name on his lips brought a faint frown to her face. He rarely ever called her by name. It was as if he threw careless endearments at her to keep her at a distance.

He pushed the damp hair back from her face. "You'll talk again," he said in an uncommonly kind tone. "And you'll sing, too, but you have to believe in yourself. Life is a challenge, Heather, not a gift. Nothing is handed to us without a little effort on our parts."

But I did work, she tried to tell him, I did, even if I had the talent to begin with, I worked to polish it! But without her voice, only her eyes could speak for her.

He searched the blue, misty depths with a quiet intensity that fanned her pulse. In the sudden silence of the room, every emotion seemed magnified. He touched her mouth with a long finger and traced, very gently, every soft curve of it. His eyes followed the movement, very narrow, very intent....

Her lips parted involuntarily under that strange gaze, her breath rushed out in a soft sigh. When his eyes darted back up to hers, something in them made her want to tear away from him and run. She'd never before felt the electricity that was gathering between then now with all the intensity of a summer storm.

"Cole..." she whispered unthinkingly, the name coming to her lips with unconscious ease. She paused, startled at the sound of her own voice.

Cole smiled. "It's taken you a long time, Heather," he said quietly.

"For...what?" she mouthed, unwilling to trust herself to speak again.

"To wonder how it would feel if I took your mouth under mine," he said.

Her cheeks flushed wildly with color as the words hit home. Suddenly everything was changed, upside down. She was being forced to admit something she'd submerged in her mind for ages—that she was aware of Cole as a man.

There was absolute stillness as two pairs of eyes met, asked questions, and waited for answers. Time hung, quivering, between them.

Chapter Three

Emma's quick step in the hall outside broke the spell. Cole released Heather with reluctance, and she avoided his eyes as she stood quietly beside the window seat.

"Here I am," Emma said with a smile, darting a quick look from her son to her stepdaughter. She didn't mention the raw tension she felt in the room as she set down a tray on the bedside table. There was a steaming cup of hot chocolate and a slice of fresh cheesecake on the tray, and Heather suddenly realized how hungry she was.

She smiled and mouthed "thank you" at the older woman, who beamed.

"Don't forget Tessa, dear," Emma told her son as she sat down in the wing chair by the bed.

"As if I could," he replied with a frankly sensual smile. Without even glancing in Heather's direction, he turned and strode with catlike grace to the door. "I think Heather's on the road to recovery. She was just able to say my name out loud," he called over his shoulder before he closed the door behind him.

Tessa. Heather felt a queer emptiness as she recalled the other girl's jet-black hair, swinging down to an impossibly narrow waist, and her black eyes that always kept the men jumping at parties. Tessa was the only daughter of a neighboring rancher, and as spoiled as a three-day-old dead fish. Anything she wanted, she got. And for years now, she'd wanted Cole.

"It's Tessa's birthday." Emma was chattering as if Heather had been paying rapt attention. "Cole's flying her to a concert in San Antonio. Poor dear, she's spent weeks choosing just the right dress."

Poor dear, indeed, Heather thought. Tessa would walk over Joan of Arc to get to Cole. And anything that threatened to take him away, even briefly, was in danger of attack. Heather's last visit home had been ruined by Tessa's jealousy. Somehow she'd managed to cheat Heather out of any time alone with Cole during the hectic three-day stopover between singing engagements.

Tessa was envious of the younger girl's career, her clothes, her beauty. She took every opportunity to throw catty remarks at her—remarks that went over Cole's head and far right of Emma's forgiving nature. It was like being clawed to death by an invisible enemy with everyone watching. Tessa had always been Heather's worst enemy. Now, at least, the younger girl knew how to protect herself. In the past, when Heather's mother was alive, she'd been more vulnerable.

Tessa had six years' advantage on the gangly child Heather had been, and in her late teens, she was unusually sophisticated for her age, just the kind of girl to appeal to a woman like Deidre Shaw. Tessa had spent more time at Big Spur than she had in her own home, and Heather had received nothing but the leftover crumbs of her mother's affection. When Deidre Shaw succumbed to pneumonia, it was Tessa she called for to nurse her. And at the funeral a few short weeks later, Heather felt as distant from her mother in death as she had in life.

Two years later Emma Everett, recently widowed herself, agreed to marry Jed Shaw and take Heather under her wing. Their families had always been close because of Jed's friendship with Big Jace Everett. With both Emma and Jed suffering the loneliness of bereavement, it seemed the most natural thing in the world for them to turn to each other. Emma and Cole were a part of Big Spur from the moment they moved in, and for the first time in her life Heather was surrounded by the warmth and affection she'd always longed for.

Cole! A tremor swept over her slender body. She'd always thought of him as her big brother. What if he did kiss her? That thought was new, and faintly shocking, as if it were forbidden to even consider any intimacy with him. But they weren't blood kin; they weren't related at all, even distantly. That made her vulnerable. It meant Cole could kiss her, touch her, and there was no reason for him to restrain himself. He could even make love to her....

Her face went scarlet. Surely her innocence would protect her—or would it? Despite the affection Cole had always felt for her, he was a man. And something she'd seen in his eyes today for the first time had convinced her that his attitude toward her had changed. Cole was the kind of man who wouldn't accept limits. He was far too experienced to revert to adolescence for the sake of a woman, and Heather didn't know how she was going to protect herself if he decided he wanted her.

With a sigh, she pulled herself up straight. All she had to go on was a new look in Cole's eyes, and she might have misread the situation entirely. Perhaps he'd only been teasing, and here she was going wild at an imagined intimacy.

She jerked her mind back to Emma's running commentary on the ranch, and her efforts to set up a day-care center for children of working mothers in the area. That was it, she'd only imagined Cole's interest. But in the back of her mind, she could still hear his male voice, quiet and dangerous, awakening dormant longings deep inside her.

Three days later, Heather was convinced that she'd imagined it all. Cole was pleasant but distant with her;

there was nothing romantic in his attitude. He didn't go out of his way to find her, but he didn't avoid her either. He was his old self, on the surface at least, and Heather began to relax as her voice and her confidence slowly returned. But sometimes she caught his silver eyes flashing toward her, and once she met a look from them that held a strange anger, almost hatred, and the intensity of it unnerved her. What had she done to make Cole dislike her so? Perhaps, she mused, he was regretting that remark he'd made and hoping she would be adult enough not to take it seriously.

Tessa swept in like a conquering army the next day, all false smiles and sweetness. She was playing up to Cole as usual while Heather sat and watched with a new emptiness in her heart.

"I was so sorry to hear about your accident." Tessa sighed, waving a perfectly manicured hand toward Heather. "You never were much of a driver, were you, darling? I remember the day you ran Cole's Ferrari through the corral fence." She laughed cuttingly, her black eyes snapping at the taller woman. "What a mess! And Cole was simply furious, weren't you, darling?" She laughed huskily, worshiping the man beside her on the couch with her eyes.

Cole smoked his cigarette silently, and his eyes narrowed, moving deliberately over Heather's slender body. She was wearing a silky beige pantsuit that hugged her slim curves like a caress.

Heather looked at his brown leather boots instead of his face, and she was alarmed at her own reaction to his blatant stare. He was only doing it to needle her, she told herself. He wasn't really interested.

Tessa continued her monologue. "We had a lovely time in San Antonio," she told the younger girl. "It was a Bach concert, so pleasant on the ears. Nothing like this vulgar modern stuff," she added with distaste. "I don't like pop music."

And that, Heather thought, was a nice dig. Just the right touch of backhanded courtesy. Tessa knew full well that Heather sang pops. Or had, until the accident.

"Have you tried singing since the accident?" Tessa asked with feigned concern. "Cole told me you're pretty nervous about how your voice will be—I guess this could mean the end of your career, couldn't it?"

Heather got up from her seat and left the room without a look or a backward glance. She was hurting too much to fight back, even if she'd had a voice to fight with.

"Oh, I shouldn't have said that, should I?" Tessa murmured, a good imitation of regret in her silky voice. "Poor little thing..."

Heather kept right on walking.

She lay awake late that night, the harsh words haunting her. Would she sing again? Did she have the courage to go back to Houston and pick up the pieces of her career? Memories of the emptiness, the loneliness, the long hours of singing in dark, smoky clubs filled her mind.

The door opened in the middle of her deep thoughts, and Cole came in, closing it behind him. He was in evening clothes, devastating in his elegant dark suit and spotless white silk shirt. His tie was off and his shirt was unbuttoned halfway down his chest, where bronzed skin and curling black hair made a dark wedge against the whiteness of the silk. He looked sublimely masculine, sensual, and Heather felt vulnerable in her frothy pink nightgown, even with the quilted coverlet pulled up over her waist. She had to fight to keep from pulling it up to her throat, especially when Cole's glittering eyes narrowed on the curves of her small, high breasts exposed by its plunging neckline.

"Couldn't sleep?" he asked quietly.

She swallowed hard and shook her tousled blond head.

He paused beside the bed, his hands on his slim hips, and stared boldly down at her.

"Nervous, honey?" he asked with amusement when she jerkily pulled up the covers.

She flushed and glared up at him.

He chuckled softly. "Little saint," he chided. "I probably know more about a woman's body than you do."

I don't doubt that for a minute, she thought furiously, and knew he could read the thought in her mind.

He reached down and touched her tousled hair tenderly. "What's the matter?" he asked quietly. "Did Tessa upset you?"

She chewed on her lower lip and averted her gaze. "Yes," she said softly.

"She doesn't understand," he reminded her. "Tessa never wanted a career. She'd rather work at being a woman."

Her eyes darted up to his curiously, searching them in the silence that followed.

His eyes narrowed at the scrutiny. "No, I don't sleep with her," he said harshly.

Her lips parted slightly as she gasped. She hadn't been wondering about that at all.

"And even if I did," he added ominously, "it wouldn't be any business of yours."

Her mouth opened, but no sound came out. She couldn't understand what had set him off.

"But then, you've never been interested in that side of my life, have you, Heather?" His silver eyes darted over her face. "You've never wondered if I had women."

That was true. But she was beginning to be curious about him in ways that shocked her.

He laughed, but without mirth. "It's just as well, little one. There wouldn't be any future in it. I've got thirteen years on you."

She'd never thought about the age difference between them before. It hadn't mattered. But suddenly it seemed to matter, to Cole anyway.

"We're going to Nassau the first of the month," he tossed out. "I need a break as much as you do, and it will do Emma good to get away from here for a while. I can spare two or three days. The sun will help you relax."

She smiled up at him. Nassau was one place she'd always wanted to see, but Cole was so busy that holidays with him were rare. Perhaps this trip would provide an opportunity to bridge the rift that was steadily growing between them.

"Lovely little girl," he murmured, looking down at her with a half-smile on his dark, hard face. "You glow when you smile at me."

Her smile widened and she reached out involuntarily to catch his hand and clasp it tightly. She felt him stiffen at the touch and draw away from her.

The smile left her face and she looked down at the coverlet with a wounded expression. She felt his silent rejection as keenly as a knife twisting inside her.

"Get some sleep, Heather," he said roughly, turning away. "Things will look better in the morning."

But they didn't. Not the next morning, or the morning after that. Cole's temper became legendary over the next few days. It was increasingly dangerous to go near him.

"I only asked him if I could drive into town," one of the cowboys moaned to Emma, "and he threw a bridle at me."

"Thank your lucky stars that there wasn't a horse attached to it," Emma told him calmly. The mischievous smile she gave him made her look twenty years younger. "You know how Cole is, Brandy."

"Yes'm," agreed the grizzled old cowboy. "But usually he only gets like this when something awful goes wrong. Like that time Moze ran the jeep over his favorite shepherd dog. Or during roundup when the calves give us fits."

"Pretend it's roundup and bear with him," Emma said in a conspiratorial whisper.

Brandy drew a long-suffering breath. "He threw a board at Herb," he muttered, turning to stride away. "Only asked could he go to Johnson's house to see his girl."

Heather smothered a smile, shaking her head.

Emma glanced at her. "You wouldn't know what's wrong with him, I suppose?" she fished.

"Ask Tessa," she returned, too quickly. "He's been like this ever since that night he took her to the country-club dance."

"That's true," Emma recalled. "But I seem to remember that he stopped by your room on his way to bed."

Heather stared at her feet. "Just to see why I was awake," she replied. It was nice to be able to talk, although she still hadn't regained full use of her voice. She hadn't dared try to sing yet. She knew it was too soon.

"He glares at you," Emma remarked. "Don't tell me you haven't noticed it."

Heather shifted from one foot to the other. "I've noticed," she admitted. His anger had hurt, too, because she didn't understand what she'd done to cause it. But she wasn't about to tell Emma that.

"He's looked after you for seven years and more," the older woman reminded her. "Now you're independent. You don't really need him anymore. He's finding that hard to accept, I think. He's very possessive of you."

"I found that out in the hospital," Heather replied with a sigh.

"So did the rest of us," Emma mused. "He went right through the ceiling when the hospital called the house and asked why he hadn't come to see about you. Poor old Bill. I don't think he's ever going to get over what Cole said to him. Cole was like a wild man that night. Do you know, he took the plane up without having it checked? That's a first."

It certainly was. But Heather didn't want to think too deeply about it. "He didn't like Gil," she murmured.

"The journalist?" Emma laughed. "You know he hates reporters. He's been hounded by them too much over the years. Maybe he thought Mr. Austin was trying to get to him through you."

She hadn't considered that. "Yes, he might have," she said, nodding.

"And, too...oh!" Emma went white and almost doubled over, sweat beading her forehead.

"Emma, what's wrong!" Heather cried, holding up her stepmother's thin form. "What is it?"

"Indigestion," came the angry, muttered reply. "Oh, it makes me so mad. I'm going to have to see a doctor eventually, but I keep thinking it'll just go away by itself.''

"Are you sure that's what it is?'' Heather studied Emma's wan face and pained expression.

Emma stood erect by herself, breathing heavily as she tried to compose herself. She managed a smile. "Yes, dear, I'm sure,'' she assured the younger woman. "Goodness, I have these attacks all the time. I just take a dose of soda or antacid and they go away. Nothing but indigestion.''

Heather's set face relaxed. She couldn't bear for anything to be wrong with Emma. It would hurt far too much to lose her.

Tessa was back the next day, clinging to Cole, and he didn't seem to mind at all. His eyes remained fixed on her slim figure, and Heather wanted to cry out. It had always bothered her to see them together, but it had never hurt like this. She was looking at Cole with new eyes now. He was powerfully built, his body every inch an athlete's. He could never have been called handsome, but his very arrogance was magnetic, and the silvery eyes under his jutting brow could charm as well as chill when he wanted them to.

He lavished charm on Tessa that evening. Linking her slender fingers with his, he gave her all his attention as they discussed business in the living room. Tessa knew as much about ranching as her father did, and she had a shrewd business sense. But right now, she was busy being a woman, and Heather felt a surge of pure jealousy in the pit of her stomach as she glanced toward the living room on her way to bed. She remembered too well the feel of Cole's fingers on her face, the sound of his deep voice. She longed for the touch of his mouth, and her own stirrings frightened her.

Jealousy like this usually accompanied love, she knew. But Cole was her stepbrother. Despite the fact that she'd always put him on a pedestal, he wasn't an object of her desire . . . or was he?

Late the next afternoon, Heather strolled out toward the corral, dressed in jeans and a soft blue cotton shirt with a deep wine pullover sweater protecting her from the chill. There were dark clouds overhead and a storm was threatening. If it had been spring or summer, she'd have sworn it was tornado weather. Even though a tornado was unlikely at this time of year, the wind was fierce.

In the corral, Cole was just swinging into the saddle of a horse Alonzo was breaking for the remuda. His tall figure was immediately recognizable as he caught the reins in one hand and ordered the men back. All at once the chestnut horse became a blur of frantic motion, but Cole's posture was faultless as he rocked with the horse, whipping back and forth in the saddle as if he'd been stuck to it with instant glue. His batwing chaps flying, he clenched his hat in one lean, powerful hand while the other controlled the furious animal. Cowboys hung on to the fence, laughing and cheering, and she could see the excitement of the challenge in Cole's hard face even at a distance. There was confidence in every line of his body, confidence coupled with a lithe grace that was blatantly masculine.

The horse gave up long before Cole and stood panting wildly, its legs trembling from exertion. Cole dismounted and gently patted the soft mane, talking to the horse in the same quiet way that he had often spoken to Heather when she was frightened.

When he saw her standing there, his face seemed to go even harder. He looked up as the first drops of rain burst out of the sky and said something to his men. Then he slammed his hat down over his eyes at its usual arrogant slant and started toward her, stripping off the batwing chaps as he walked. He held them over one arm and caught her around the waist with the other, herding her toward the nearby barn as the sky opened up and dumped a spray of liquid bullets onto them.

"You can't afford a chill right now," he shot at her. "Run, girl!"

She raced beside him, exhilarated even as his long legs easily outdistanced her. When they reached the barn, her face was flushed, her eyes laughing, her hair in a glorious tumble. Inside, two rows of neat stalls were separated by a long aisle filled with fresh honey-colored wood shavings that made a cushion on the hard ground. She pushed her hair out of her blue eyes and laughed up at Cole as they stood by the door, watching the cold rain pelt down on the paddocks between the barn and the house.

His eyes flicked over her and moved away, back to the rain. He tossed the chaps and his hat aside, idly reaching in his pocket for a cigarette. She watched him light it, her eyes drawn to his strong, tanned fingers as they worked the lighter. The nails were flat and clean, despite the manual labor he occasionally engaged in.

"I didn't know you still rode broncs," she said, breaking the tense silence.

"There are a lot of things you don't know about me," he replied without looking at her. He leaned against the barn wall and stared out at the rain with narrowed gray eyes.

That was true. Cole had always been something of a mystery: a secretive, very private person who allowed no one, not even his stepsister, too close.

"Cole, what have I done?" she asked suddenly, unable to bear his coolness a second longer.

He still didn't look at her. "What makes you think you've done anything?"

She lowered her eyes to the ground and moved the wood shavings around lightly with the toe of her boot. "I don't know... you're very distant with me lately."

He laughed mirthlessly, with a sound that was as harsh as the rapping of the rain on the roof or the rumble of thunder.

"Don't laugh," she murmured. "We were always close, even when we argued. But it's all changed now, and I don't understand why."

He took a long draw from the cigarette. The howl of the wind echoed through the cozy warmth of the barn; the thunder made the ground shiver. Without warning, his eyes came around to pierce hers, and the intensity of his gaze made her want to back away. "You made the choice, not me," he said roughly.

She blinked at him. "What choice?"

"To turn your back on your family and carve out a career for yourself," he said coldly.

She felt shivers run down her arms and she averted her eyes. "You'll never forgive me for that, will you? It was the first time in my life I ever went against you, and you'll die remembering." She shook back her hair angrily. "I worshiped you, Cole!" she threw at him, her eyes half-hurt, half-angry.

His jaw went taut. "When will you understand that I don't want hero worship from you?" he shot at her.

Her lower lip pouted at him. "What do you want?" she challenged.

He threw the cigarette outside into the rain and moved toward her before she could read the intent in his glittering eyes. She shrank back against the rough boards as he propped his lean, brown hands on the wall on either side of her head and eased his body completely down against hers, pinning her there in a silence that burned with emotion. She felt his chest, warm and hard through the layers of clothing, pressing against her soft breasts, his flat stomach and powerful legs in intimate contact with her own.

"Let me show you what I want," he growled, and what she read in his eyes made her pulse run wild with frightened anticipation.

"Cole...you can't!" she whispered shakily, her eyes wide and bright.

His eyes dropped to her soft mouth. "Why can't I?" he challenged. "You've done everything but go down on your knees and beg me for it since you came out of the hospital."

She opened her mouth to deny it, and his dark head bent swiftly. He caught her parted lips with his own, and she felt their rough, demanding warmth for the first time. Her body went rigid as he twisted her lips roughly under his, not a trace of gentleness in him. He was angry and the kiss was the medium of that anger. She moaned weakly under the painful crush of his mouth, his body.

He drew back, breathing hard, his eyes blazing straight into hers from a distance of inches. He studied her tear-bright eyes mercilessly. "How does it feel?" he demanded gruffly.

Her lips trembled. "I . . . I don't know," she whispered, shaken by the close contact with his powerful, hard-muscled body, by the scent of tobacco and oriental cologne that clung to him, by the lingering taste of his mouth.

"You wanted it," he accused, something violent in the flash of his eyes.

Her breath caught on a sob. "Not anymore," she got out. "Please let me go."

He hesitated an instant before he shoved himself away from her and stepped back. His eyes surveyed the damage, the tears shining beneath her eyelashes, the sudden pallor of her face. Then she darted out the door into the storm, oblivious to the driving rain that drenched her before she reached the safety of the house. She was equally oblivious to the narrowed gray eyes that watched her every step of the way.

Chapter Four

Heather pleaded a headache and avoided going to the supper table, thankful that Emma didn't pursue her with tablets or questions. She didn't know that the older woman had immediately spotted the heightened color of her face and the shocked confusion in her eyes.

She went straight up to her own room to lock herself in and stare dumbfounded at the image in her mirror. Her face was a stranger's, with its wide, blue eyes and wildly flushed cheeks. Her mouth had a suddenly passionate look about it, and even now she could taste the smoky warmth of Cole's mouth with her tongue.

Her eyes closed against the image. Her body could still feel the powerful crush of his. She'd never realized before just how strong he really was. No amount of effort on her part would have freed her—despite the fact that she'd been too shocked to struggle. And he'd had the audacity to say she'd tempted him!

Tempted him, indeed! As if she would have dared to measure her inexperience against his expertise. Not even a novice could have come out of those powerful arms ignorant of the fact that he'd had women. Despite his anger, he had been devastatingly expert. She was grateful that he hadn't been persuasive as well, because she'd never have been able to resist him.

She folded her arms around her shivering body and went to the window to watch the rain come down. Had she tempted him? If looking at him or touching him was temptation, why hadn't this happened years ago? She sighed, shaking her tousled head. He'd always known that she put him on a pedestal in her mind. Why had he suddenly decided to come tumbling down from it?

The questions nagged at her far into the night. She wanted to run, like a calf faced with a branding iron. She was afraid of Cole in a new and exciting way. She'd seen him as a lover, and it frightened her to be vulnerable to him.

She thought about leaving Big Spur to go back to Houston. She could call one of her many contacts in the entertainment world and try to line up a job. But was that what she really wanted? She hadn't yet tested her singing voice and she knew that her hesitancy came from a reluctance to make any hard and fast decisions about her career. It was her singing that had caused the breach between her and Cole—should she continue to pursue it despite his objections?

She had already begun to question herself about her career before the accident. Now those doubts returned to haunt her.

In her weakened state, how would she adjust to the exhausting pace of an engagement schedule? Two shows a night, every night, six days a week, and constant rehearsals. And how would she fight the overwhelming loneliness that assailed her every time she ran away from Big Spur and Cole?

She went down the stairs reluctantly the next morning, dressed in jeans and a soft yellow V-necked sweater, her hair in a sophisticated French twist at the back of her long, graceful neck. She was hoping against hope that Cole would be off on another trip, or downtown at his business office in Branntville.

But he was still at the breakfast table, alone and brooding. His fingers toyed with a coffee cup that was obviously empty. His dark hair was unruly over his jutting brow, his burgundy shirt open at the throat and straining across the powerful muscles of his chest. He looked forbidding, and Heather paused uncertainly in the doorway, her mind urging retreat.

As if he sensed her presence, he looked up, and something flashed in his silver eyes like summer lightning.

The events of the day before stood between them, the memory of them coming alive as her eyes went involuntarily to his hard mouth. She vividly remembered the crush of his lips against hers. She even remembered the scent of him, the clean warmth of his face, the feel of his body....

"You might as well come in," he said in a curt, angry tone. "It won't go away."

She lifted her face proudly and refused to be drawn into asking him what he meant. She sat down two chairs away from him and reached for the coffeepot. Her fingers trembled slightly as she filled a cup. "Where's Emma?" she asked, trying to make idle conversation.

"Gone into town to see the doctor," he replied curtly.

She frowned. "Is there something wrong?" she asked in concern.

Cole shook his head. "It's just that indigestion she's been complaining of lately—I finally convinced her to see the doctor about it." His eyes shot to her face, cutting and hard. "Now, are there any other topics you'd like to cover before we discuss what's really on both our minds?"

She stared at the reflection of the chandelier in her black coffee. "I don't want to talk about it, Cole," she said in a low voice.

He drew a short breath and lit a cigarette with quick jerky movements. He took a draw from it before he looked up, and his gaze didn't miss the dark circles under her eyes. "Did I hurt you, Heather?" he asked in a tone that she'd never heard him use before.

Her cheeks went dusky pink, and she could only manage to shake her head.

He murmured something harsh under his breath before he leaned back in the chair with a violent motion, throwing one muscular arm over the back of it so that his shirt was stretched taut over his broad, hair-shadowed chest. His eyes narrowed as he took another draw from the cigarette and expelled it forcefully. "Will you look at me, damn it?"

Her eyes jerked up apprehensively. Everything she felt, the confusion and the hurt, showed in her face.

"Didn't you realize," he said quietly, "that every look you've given me lately has been an open invitation? We've lived like brother and sister for the past seven years, but the fact remains that there isn't a drop of blood between us. We don't even share a mutual cousin. There's nothing to stop me, Heather."

She averted her eyes to the colorful arrangement of mums on the table and she swallowed hard. "I... wasn't trying to... to tempt you," she said. "I've looked at you... like I always have."

"No," he said.

Her eyes flashed at him. "I'll wear blinders from now on, that's for sure," she threw back.

"Afraid of me?" he asked with a slow, sensual smile.

"Terrified!" she replied.

He finished the cigarette and crushed it out in the ashtray beside his plate. "Why, because I hurt you?"

"You weren't gentle," she said in a subdued tone.

His eyes caught hers. "I'm not a gentle man. I'm hot-blooded and I like my women the same way. I've never made love to an adolescent before. I was rough with you because I'm used to women who know the rules. You don't."

Her face was the color of a boiled beet when he got through. Her pride was in shreds as she glared at him. "I'm not an adolescent!"

"You kiss like one."

Her eyes flashed blue sparks at him, and he smiled lazily at the indignation in them.

"That wasn't a kiss," she returned furiously. "It was an assault!"

He threw back his head and laughed, the sound of it deep and pleasant and maddening.

"Well, it was!" she grumbled, toying with her coffee cup.

"Have you ever been made love to properly?" he asked with a gleam in his eye.

She avoided his patient stare. "What's that got to do with it?" she asked uneasily.

"A lot. Apparently you're used to men who'll settle for light pecks on the lips and an occasional embrace." His eyes dropped to her mouth. "I like my kisses hard and rough and deep. I like to feel a woman's body against every inch of mine."

"So I noticed," she said, trying to ignore the wave of embarrassment that swept over her.

"Did you? You were standing there so rigid you felt like stone. If you'd let that soft young body relax against mine, it wouldn't have hurt." One corner of his chiseled mouth went up in a wicked smile. "You might even have enjoyed it."

"Cole!" she gasped, outraged.

He chuckled, pushing back his chair. "We'll try it again when you grow up a little," he said, lifting an arrogant eyebrow at her as he started out of the room. "I don't like making love to children."

"You . . . egomaniacal *beast!*" she ground out.

But he only kept walking. She drained her coffee cup with a furious disregard for the temperature of the coffee, so angry she wanted to throw things. No other man had ever inspired in her the violence of emotion that Cole did. He could make her feel positively murderous.

"I see flames rising from your hair," Emma remarked as Heather joined her in the living room later that afternoon.

"I want to burn Cole at the stake," she said without thinking.

"What's he done now?" the older woman asked with amusement in her dark eyes.

"What hasn't he done!" Heather's blue eyes burned. "He's the most maddening, irritating man I've ever known!"

"Fire and ice," Emma agreed with a tender smile, "just like his father. Jason was that way, too."

Heather studied the softness in the other woman's face as she spoke. "You loved him very much, didn't you?"

The brown eyes were wistful. "All the way to my soul. It very nearly killed me when he died. Cole was the only reason I didn't throw myself over a cliff. Oh, your father was a great comfort to me in later years, but Jason was...everything."

"Did he look like Cole?" she asked.

"Exactly. He was a handsome devil, all right. Always had women chasing him—even after we were married! Why, your own mother used to flirt with him outrageously. It didn't bother me, though. Jason never had eyes for anyone but me."

"Where did you meet him?"

"At a rodeo." Emma laughed. "He was one of the suppliers, and my brother was riding one of the broncs he supplied. I looked at him and I knew I'd die if I couldn't have him. He must have felt the same way—" she sighed "—because we married six days later."

"My goodness!" Heather gasped. She and Emma had never talked about Cole's father until now, and she was fascinated. "Talk about whirlwind courtships!"

"It was crazy, all right, but Jason always did impulsive things. Like riding that bronc..." The light in her eyes seemed to go out, like a candle extinguished by a strong, bitter wind.

"Tell me how your day-care center is going," Heather said quickly, changing the subject.

Emma's face brightened again as she launched into the details of her latest project.

* * *

The tension between Cole and Heather was almost palpable, and Emma glanced suspiciously from one to the other at the supper table. "It's cold out today," she said finally.

"Arctic," Cole agreed with a glance. "We're going to Nassau in the morning."

"In the morning!" Emma burst out. "But we haven't even packed . . . !"

"To hell with packing," he growled. "Buy what you need when we get there. I'm not dragging along a truckload of suitcases."

Heather stared at him in bewilderment. "You said we'd go the first of the month," she murmured.

His eyes narrowed on her face. "And I've changed my mind. Did you have any other plans . . . like visiting that damned reporter?"

She gaped at him. "You told Gil he couldn't come here," she reminded him.

"That wouldn't stop you from running to him behind my back to spite me," he growled.

Emma started to intercede when the doorbell rang and Mrs. Jones went ambling past the dining room to answer it. A moment later they heard Tessa's high voice in the hall.

Just what I need, Heather thought viciously, dropping her eyes to her plate as the dark-haired girl whirled into the room, a vision in pale blue chiffon so simply cut that it must have cost a fortune.

"Supper! How lovely, I've just gotten back from Miami and I haven't had a bite." She sighed, easing a chair closer to Cole's and motioning for Mrs. Jones to bring her a place setting. "You don't mind, do you, darling?" she asked Cole confidently.

"Help yourself," he said with a distant smile. "How was Miami?"

"Hot," came the indifferent reply.

"I'm looking forward to some heat, too," Emma sighed. "I only hope Nassau isn't in the path of that hurricane they're tracking."

"Nassau?" Tessa looked suddenly like a dog hot on the trail of a juicy bone. "Are you going there?"

"I'm flying them down tomorrow," Cole said, his eyes on Heather's downcast face. "We need a change of scene."

"May I hitch a ride with you?" Tessa asked quickly. "Uncle James lives there, you know, and I've been meaning to visit him for months now. I was going to book a commercial flight in a few weeks, but it would be much more fun to fly down with you...." She looked up at Cole coquettishly.

He was watching the stillness of Heather's face like a hawk, and his eyes grew calculating. "Come along, by all means," he said. "The Cessna's plenty big enough."

"Thank you, darling," Tessa purred, ignoring the other two women as she edged even closer to Cole.

Heather stabbed her piece of steak with a jerk of her wrist that didn't go unnoticed by a pair of silver eyes.

Tessa left after supper to hurry home and pack, and Emma pleaded fatigue soon afterwards. Cole had withdrawn to his den to go over some paperwork, leaving Heather to say good night to Mrs. Jones and turn off the lights on her way to the staircase.

She reached the first step and had her hand on the bannister when Cole's deep voice called to her.

"I want to talk to you for a minute," he said, turning back into the firelit room, confident that she'd be right behind him.

And she was, glaring at his broad back in exasperation. He was wearing a pale yellow shirt that emphasized his darkness and dark slacks that clung to the powerful lines of his thighs. He perched on the edge of his desk with a smoking cigarette in his hand and stared at her.

She hadn't realized how the aqua knit pantsuit she was wearing clung to her soft curves until she noticed the way his silvery eyes were tracing her body. She wished she'd worn something a little less revealing.

"Close the door," he said quietly.

She glanced at it and then back at him. "Why?" she wanted to know.

His eyes narrowed. "Because I'm going to throw you down on that rug in front of the fire and make passionate love to you, that's why," he growled.

She shifted restlessly, turning away from his sarcastic voice to close the door very gently. "You don't have to make fun of me."

"You do a lot for my ego," he remarked.

She glanced at him nervously. "You've already got more women than you know what to do with," she said, trying to make a joke out of it. "Aren't you chased enough?"

"I like to do the chasing," he replied. His eyes narrowed. "I'm old-fashioned that way."

"I'm not fair game, you know," she told him, licking her lips uneasily.

"Because you're a novice?" he asked, and his eyes swept over her flushed face as he said it. "I didn't allow for that, did I? I took for granted that you had a little experience to draw on."

"I've never felt like experimenting," she said quietly, moving to ease down into the red leather armchair beside the desk.

"No sex, in other words."

She hated the color that flamed again in her cheeks. "Stop making me feel inadequate," she choked. "If I'm repressed, you have to take some of the blame, Cole. I always got the feeling that you'd beat anyone who tried to take advantage of me."

"I would have," he admitted arrogantly. "I've never liked the idea of men pawing you."

"What would you call what you were doing to me?" she challenged hotly.

A corner of his mouth curled. "Disastrous," he said dryly.

Her eyes fell to her lap. "Don't let's be like this, Cole," she said after a minute, her face drawn as she lifted it again. "I can't bear having you angry with me. I don't feel welcome here anymore."

He studied her through a screen of gray smoke and sighed. "Do you really think we can go back seven years and start over?"

She stared at the hand-carved wood of the mantel. "Nothing happened," she said stubbornly.

"Nothing?" he asked in a deep, lazy tone.

She swallowed, glancing at him and away. "Almost nothing," she amended.

She heard him move before she looked up and found him standing over her. He placed one brown hand on the arm of the chair and leaned over, looking straight into her wavering eyes. "I want you," he said quietly, studying the shock that froze her face.

Had she heard him right? Her eyes dilated wildly.

"Now that I have your complete attention," he added dryly, "let's get something straight. Despite the fact that I don't feel particularly brotherly toward you, I do have some protective instincts left. You're twenty, and damned easy on the eyes, and you're blessed with the sexiest body I've ever touched. I may be thirteen years your senior, but I am neither blind nor impotent, and if you don't start treating me like the threat to your honor I could become, you are going to find yourself in one hell of a mess very soon."

She stared at him like a statue, her lips slightly parted, her senses numb.

"I'm a man," he continued. "Don't you know the effect those bedroom eyes of yours have? You haven't looked at me since you've been out of the hospital without staring quite pointedly at my mouth. You touch me like a fawn asking to be petted. You tremble all over when I come near you. Those are signals that no man misses, Heather, and you've been sending them constantly for almost a year. The only thing that's saved you so far is the fact that you haven't been home very often."

"I . . . I didn't realize . . . !" she said honestly.

He drew erect with a hard sigh. "I'm not immune to you," he said quietly. "I thought I was, but I'm not. What happened in the barn wasn't something I planned, but it was almost inevitable. And if you don't watch your step, it might not be an isolated incident."

"I'll wear a sack over my head and never look at you again," she muttered sulkily.

He caught her wrist and jerked her out of the chair with sudden violence, whipping her against his hard frame with devastating strength. He stared down into her eyes with a dangerous glitter in his.

"Cole . . . !" she gasped.

"I'm not playing games," he said tightly. "You may not think I'm a threat, but I could prove to you that I am."

She swallowed her fear and forced herself to stand still. She knew instinctively that it would be stupid to fight him.

"I believe you," she said carefully.

"No, you don't," he replied, eyeing her soft mouth. "You think the only thing you have to worry about is getting a bruised mouth. It isn't. This . . ." he murmured, tilting her face up to his with hard, warm fingers, "is what you have to worry about."

His mouth nibbled gently at hers in the sudden, breathless silence that followed, and she felt his tongue tracing a sensuous pattern between her trembling lips. His teeth nipped tenderly at her lower lip as his hands smoothed the blouse against her spine, lazily caressing, coaxing her body gently to him until her breasts melted against the warm strength of his chest.

She caught her breath, her eyes slitted, and she watched his chiseled lips lift and brush against her mouth.

"Closer," he whispered sensually, letting his hands slide down to her hips and urge them toward his to make an intimate contact that she should have protested.

Her hands trembled on his chest. "Cole, I..." she said shakily.

His mouth nudged her lips apart and bit at them. "Open your mouth," he whispered. "A kiss can be as intimate as making love. Let me show you...."

The funny little moan that tore out of her throat shocked her. She'd never dreamed that people kissed like this, touched like this. His mouth was taking possession of hers, and she was letting it, without a single protest.

Her hands flattened against his chest, feeling the warmth of it, the strength of it, while he took what he wanted from her yielding lips.

"Unbutton it," he murmured against her mouth. "Put your hands on my chest and touch me."

"Cole..."

He drew back and looked into her misty eyes. His own were smoldering. "Is that too intimate?" he asked quietly.

She fought to catch her breath. She could feel the hard slam of his heartbeat under her fingers; she could actually hear the pounding of her own in her throat.

"It...isn't fair," she whispered weakly. "You know I'm no match for you. You know too much."

"Do you want me to stop?" he asked curtly.

"Yes." Her eyes closed and she bit her lip to stem the tears. It hurt her pride to realize how little resistance she had.

His hands contracted for an instant before he released her completely and moved away to the bar. He poured himself a glass of whiskey and took two deep swallows of it, his back to her. He took a long, harsh breath without turning. "Go to bed, little girl," he said roughly.

That hurt, as he meant it to. She stared helplessly at his broad back. "What do you want from me, Cole?" she asked in a voice that trembled despite her best efforts to control it.

"Nothing," he ground out. "Not a damned thing. Go to bed."

She started to pursue it, but she knew it wouldn't be any use. His back was as rigid as a poker, just as rigid as his will. She'd never understand him.

Her hand closed on the doorknob.

"Heather?"

"What?" she asked tightly.

"Don't ever let me get that close again unless you're ready to deal with the consequences."

She opened the door and went out, closing it firmly behind her.

The trip to Nassau was agonizing. Tessa sat in the cockpit with Cole all the way, playing up to him with practiced skill. And Cole seemed to enjoy it, his manner possessive, his smile easy. He'd barely spared Heather a glance since they started out, and when he had, his look was condemning. As if it was her fault that he'd kissed her...!

Her eyes closed at the sensual memory. It made her blush just to think about the touch of his mouth on hers, the feel of his hands, his whispered words. She'd never felt desire before, but it was no stranger anymore. She knew what it was to burn with longing, to feel her body alive and tense and aching. If Cole hadn't stopped, she'd never have been able to stop him. Anything he'd wanted from her, he could have taken, and they both knew it. But what did he want? Why was he so hateful? She hadn't tempted him on purpose, but he was acting as if she had. Everything was different between them now, everything. She wanted to go back, but all the doors were suddenly closed. There was no way but forward, and she was afraid of the future.

"You're very quiet," Emma said as they landed on the lovely Caribbean island.

"The trip has tired me out," Heather said sweetly. "It's a long way."

"So it is," Emma agreed. She patted Heather's slender hand. "We'll have a rest when we get to our hotel. You'll feel better after a nap."

"Of course," Heather agreed, but the smile she gave didn't reach her eyes.

Heather leaned over the balcony of the hotel room she was sharing with Emma and stared out across the bay with its shimmering aqua water and bleached white beach. She breathed in the luscious fragrance of sea and sun and bougainvillea, her hair lifting in the moist, sultry breeze. The island was everything she'd dreamed it would be.

There were plenty of restaurants and hotels nearby, but Heather didn't feel any more like nightclubbing that first night than Emma did, so they stayed behind while Cole took Tessa out on the town. Heather felt a rage that was just barely concealed as she watched them leave the hotel. Cole was so handsome, so masculine in evening clothes, and Tessa's figure in a slinky black sequined dress was incredibly alluring. How could Cole resist the invitation it made? Remembering the delicious roughness of his mouth on hers, Heather couldn't bear the certainty that Tessa would know it before the evening was over. All that powerful masculinity taking possession of her senses, drowning her in pleasure....

She went back inside the room, and got into her nightgown without disturbing Emma, who was already asleep. But it was hours before Heather, too, fell into uneasy dreams.

* * *

Emma was no swimmer, and she was equally leery of sunbathing, so she decided to go shopping instead of joining Heather for breakfast and a morning on the beach.

"You go ahead, dear," she said, smiling as she slid on her sunglasses. "I'm sorry you won't have company. Tessa's uncle *would* decide to go to France on the spur of the moment and close up his house. I suppose it was hard for Cole to say no when she asked him to tour her around the island."

That bit of information had only come out this morning and it had hit Heather like a bucket of wet cement. Now she found she was jealous in a way she'd never thought she could be. She wanted to rip Tessa's hair out by the roots. "I'll be all right," she said quietly.

Emma watched her intently as she nodded. "Don't forget to use that sunscreen we brought along," she cautioned. "And wear sunglasses. This is a subtropical island, and the sun is very strong."

"I'll remember. Have a good time."

"You, too." Emma touched her arm affectionately. "Tessa's a habit, Heather," she added with amazing insight. "Don't give up."

She flushed wildly as she met the older woman's eyes. "What do you mean?"

Emma smiled secretively. "I remember Cole's father very well, you know," was all she said, but when she left the spacious room, Heather had the feeling that Emma was very aware of everything that was going on around her.

The arcade adjoining their hotel was lined with expensive shops and several restaurants. A few minutes after Emma left, Heather went down to get her breakfast. She was wearing an attractive blue and aqua patterned shirtwaist dress and strappy sandals, and her long blond hair blew around her shoulders in the breeze.

She felt deserted somehow. Not that she minded Emma going out on her own. But Cole had been all but avoiding her, ever since that night in the study. She grimaced, remembering her own cowardice. But she'd been afraid of him. Cole was a man, after all, and he'd admitted that he didn't recognize limits with a woman. Heather, for all her beauty and surface sophistication, was still innocent in the ways of passion, and Cole terrified her. All he had to do was kiss her in that arrogant, intimate way and she'd give him anything he wanted. She sighed wistfully. Probably he knew that. It would explain why he was deliberately keeping a distance between them.

Or maybe he just preferred Tessa. Heather's blue eyes clouded. All her life, it seemed, Tessa had taken away the things that mattered most: Heather's mother, Heather's boyfriends, even a beautiful emerald bracelet that Deidre Shaw had given to Tessa despite the fact that it had been willed to Heather by a great aunt. And now Tessa was going to get Cole, too.

Heather went into a little coffee shop on the arcade and ordered a danish and coffee, watching as her five-dollar bill was changed and she was given three colorful Bahamian one-dollar bills and some oddly beautiful Bahamian coins. Except for the musical accents of the Bahamian personnel who operated the coffee shop, and the funny little foreign cars and wildly careening jitneys going down the side street at the back of the restaurant, she might have been in any large American city.

She stirred her coffee restlessly. Why was Cole avoiding her? Or was Tessa's harassing presence only making it seem as though he was? Annoyed at the turn her thoughts had taken, she ignored them while she finished her breakfast. Later, reclining in a comfortable beach chair under a palm-roofed umbrella, she watched a passenger ship leave port. It was flying a British flag, and the railings were lined with tourists watching the small fishing boats come and go. Heather had already seen the two small tugboats turn the huge ocean liner around and she had been fascinated by the process. The passenger ships were unlike anything she'd ever seen, and she wondered idly where the people on them were going and if any of them were as lonely as she was.

"You're all alone?" a pleasant voice asked at her shoulder.

She half swiveled in her chair, aware of the brevity of her yellow bikini and the very interested stare of the dark-haired, dark-eyed man standing at her side. "Not quite," she said dryly, motioning toward the fifty other people scattered over the beach.

He laughed delightedly and shook his head. "I have, how you say, the wrong phrase. American?"

She nodded. "French?" she probed.

He shrugged. "It is my accent. And I thought my English was *magnifique!*"

"Oh, it is," she assured him, liking his breezy, friendly manner.

"Are you here with someone?" he asked, both dark brows lifted over his dancing dark eyes.

"Yes, I am." She watched his face fall and laughed. "My stepmother," she added, and the smile came back.

"I may join you?" he asked hopefully.

"It isn't a very big chair," she remarked wryly.

He chuckled delightedly and went to get his own beach chair. He was tall, but not thin, and not bad-looking either in his sky-blue trunks. He had thrown a matching towel carelessly around his shoulders and was wearing a gold serpentine chain around his neck that looked very expensive. She was sure the diamond on his small finger was real.

"You do not wish to lie in the sun?" he asked, curious.

"I burn," she told him. "It's safer here in the shade, and much, much cooler."

"The water is cool," he remarked, turning to lie on his side and study her.

"Not terribly, but it is very salty." She sighed. "Like the drinking water here," she added with a laugh.

"My first taste of it was an experience. And can you believe there's a water shortage in the city, with the whole Caribbean and Atlantic all around!"

"You should drink bottled water," he advised. "Much nicer to the taste."

"So they say, but I'd rather drink the Goombay punch."

"You are a model?" he asked.

"A singer," she corrected.

"*C'est vrai?* How marvelous! You sing here, on the island?"

"No, back in the States. Or I did, until I was in a wreck. My voice is just now coming back," she explained. "What do you do?" she added.

"I write," he said. "Adventure novels mostly, but I'm on vacation this week. I have, how you say, a tired brain." He chuckled.

"Mine stays that way." She studied his lean face. "You don't look like a writer," she remarked absently.

He grinned. "You do not look like a singer so much as like a cover girl. If I am not too presumptuous, are you busy this evening?" He reached out a finger and traced a pattern lightly on her cheek. "I would like to show you the night life at the casino." He grinned. "Gambling is exciting."

"And sometimes extremely dangerous," came a deep, angry voice behind Heather.

She turned and looked straight up into a pair of blazing silver eyes that could belong to only one man.

Chapter Five

She stared blankly at Cole as the other man hastily excused himself. Cole's shirt was open completely over his broad, bronzed chest with its wedge of dark hair. He looked completely masculine and she studied him silently for several seconds before she realized how uncovered she herself was. His gaze had dropped deliberately to her body, clothed only in the tiny bikini, her small, high breasts emphasized by the cut of the suit. The Frenchman's glance hadn't disturbed her a great deal, but Cole's was devastating. She felt as though his hard fingers were touching her body.

With a jerky movement, she reached for her beach jacket and quickly pulled it on, buttoning it up the front.

"Planning to go into burlesque, Heather?" he asked with an icy note in his voice that roused her temper.

"No, I'm not!" She squared her shoulders, forgetting her embarrassment in a flash of indignation. "I'm not thirteen anymore, and I won't let you tell me how to dress!"

"Oh no?" he asked with a mocking smile. He reached out unexpectedly and jerked her to her feet. Despite her struggles, he held her wrist in an unshakable clasp and half pulled, half dragged her along the sand toward the hotel, leaving her beach towel behind.

She gasped, trying to fight, but she hadn't taken his strength into account. All those years of backbreaking work on the ranch had given him steely muscles. Cole had never been the desk tycoon many wealthy men were. He kept his powerful, athletic body in fighting trim, and at times like this, he was unbeatable.

"Let me go!" she burst out. "Cole, I'll never forgive you...."

"You're making a scene," he cautioned.

"I don't care!" she flashed back. But she did. The warning hushed her as effectively as a gag.

He reached the door to her room, threw it open, and hurled her inside, pausing to slam the door behind them.

She rubbed her wrist with a wounded expression. "What would you have done if I hadn't left the door unlocked?" she asked in a thin, sarcastic tone.

"Kicked it down," he replied coolly, and she didn't doubt that he would have.

"It's my body," she said unsteadily.

"Not to flaunt in front of every man on the make," he replied curtly. He fished out a cigarette and lit it without taking his glittering eyes from her.

"I'm a grown woman!" she returned.

"Only from the neck down!" he shot at her, his eyes dangerous. "Is modesty passé in your generation?"

"You're just old-fashioned," she accused.

"Damned right," he agreed, drawing on his cigarette. "I believe in modesty and I'll want a virgin when I marry."

"Will Tessa still be one by then?" she asked sweetly, folding her arms across her chest.

"Tessa is none of your business, little miss," he reminded her.

"And I'm none of yours, Cole!"

"You are until you reach twenty-one."

"For Heaven's sake!" she exclaimed, exasperated. She slung back her long platinum hair, and her blue eyes met his accusingly. "If you'd only stop treating me like a child...."

"That Frenchman wouldn't have treated you like one," he reminded her with narrowed eyes.

"Were you jealous?" she threw at him without thinking.

"Yes," he said incredibly, his face taut. "I don't want other men looking at you like that." His gaze traveled slowly down her body. "You belong to me. Every inch of you. And I don't intend sharing you with Austin, some damned Frenchman, or anyone else."

She caught her breath at his words, unsure if he was joking or not.

"I . . . I'm not a possession," she managed lightly, trying to treat his remark as a jest.

His eyes narrowed. "You're going to be," he said softly. He paused to crush his cigarette out in an ashtray on the chest of drawers. And then he moved toward her, sensual, deliberately making her aware of every step he took. Her lips parted, her eyes yielded before he ever reached her, her body faintly tingling, hungry. . . .

"Well, hello!" Emma called suddenly, breezing into the room with a basketful of shopping treasures, her glance darting belatedly to the tableau by the window. Her eyes twinkled under the brim of the pretty hat she'd bought as she studied their rigid stances.

"Did I interrupt World War Three?" she teased.

"One of the primary skirmishes," Cole said nonchalantly. His eyes flicked over Heather carelessly, as if nothing at all had happened. "Tell this stupid child why she can't parade around half-naked in front of the beach wolves," he told his mother. "She won't listen to me."

He was out the door and gone before Heather could think of a suitable reply. First she had to get her pulse and her breathing back to some semblance of normality. She felt as if her knees were about to buckle under her.

"I hate him!" she breathed, her cheeks flushed, her legs visibly trembling.

Emma put her parcels down and sat in one of the comfortable chairs with the colorful hat at a jaunty angle atop her silvery hair. "Tell me about it," she prompted.

Heather dropped down onto the bed, folding her hands in her lap. "He won't let me out on the beach."

"He won't?"

"Not in this bikini," Heather amended. "Oh, Emma, why is he so repressed?" she groaned.

"Because he gets homicidal when other men look at you fully clothed, much less like that," came the calm, amused reply.

Heather looked surprised. "Cole?"

"Cole." Emma smiled at the younger woman, her brown eyes twinkling. "He doesn't want men looking at you, much less touching you. Do you know what he said about your friend Gil Austin? That he was going to break up your friendship with him any way he could." She laughed at Heather's blank stare. "Which means that he doesn't like the idea of you and Mr. Austin together. He's jealous."

"There's Tessa...."

"Who runs after Cole, not the reverse."

"Nobody forces him to date her."

"Don't you, my darling?" the older woman asked gently.

Heather gaped at her. "I do?"

"You do everything but dive under the furniture when Cole walks into the room," she remarked, studying Heather's face. "You snap at him all the time. You push him away as if you're terrified to let him come close. Which I imagine you are," she added quietly. "Isn't that the truth?"

Heather drew in a shaky breath. "I love you very much, but I'm not ready to talk about it, not yet. Anyway, Cole's the one who jumps on me."

"He wouldn't if you'd walk toward him for a change," Emma advised. "You've always dressed up for people like Gil Austin. Tonight, why not try, just once, dressing to please Cole? Why not try treating him the way Tessa does for a change and see what happens?"

"He'd just slap me down." Heather pouted. "He doesn't even like me to touch him."

"My darling, don't you even know why?" Emma asked gently. She turned away with a smile. "You never know the rewards until you're willing to take the risks."

Heather stared after her for a long time, her mind whirling.

It was new, and exciting, to think about deliberately trying to catch Cole's eye. Never before in their turbulent relationship had she tried to use her wiles on him. But remembering the flames dancing in his eyes when he'd looked at her on the beach, she began to think about what Emma had told her. Cole had looked as if he wanted to throttle the Frenchman just for staring at her. That kind of murderous fury went beyond simple affection. "You belong to me," he'd said.

She was just beginning to understand what he'd meant.

It was still hard to believe he'd really said that, even now, as she eased the delicious black designer dress over her head. It had a halter neck and was cut below the waist in back, a dream in silky Qiana, all black with glorious patches of vivid yellow flowers. With her fair coloring and long blond hair, it was achingly beautiful. She wore tiny black suede sandals with small spiked heels and a yellow flower over one ear. Emma, dressed in a long blue chiffon confection that made her dark eyes darker, stood and shook her head wonderingly when she saw Heather.

"Poor Cole," she murmured wickedly.

"I . . . it's old," came the embarrassed reply.

"Oh, at least two weeks old, I'm sure." Emma laughed. "Come on. I can't wait to see Tessa's face."

Heather nervously clutched her tiny black evening bag as she followed Emma into the combination restaurant and lounge where Cole and Tessa were talking at a candlelit corner table overlooking the dark Caribbean.

Cole was devastating in his dark evening clothes, his hair gleaming in the muted light from the ceiling. He was so ruggedly handsome he caused Heather's pulse to race. If Heather had dressed to the hilt, Tessa wasn't far behind. She was wearing a frothy white creation with a ruffle edging the neckline that plunged all the way down to a daring front slit. It was all held together by a wide white belt, and Heather had a suspicion that without the belt, the two edges of the dress would part company. The effect of the white dress contrasting with Tessa's snapping dark eyes and dark hair was dramatic.

Two pairs of eyes looked up when Emma and Heather made their way to the table. Tessa's were openly hostile. In the stunning black and yellow dress, Heather was as eye-catching as a tropical bird, and Tessa's jealousy was written in her black eyes. Cole's gaze was harder to read. He rose to his feet slowly, his eyes never leaving Heather. They ran over her like a caress, but his face was as steely as ever, giving nothing away as he seated the two women.

"What a lovely dress," Tessa said with a sweet smile. "Make it yourself?"

Heather returned her smile. "My little old dress designer did," she replied. "Get yours off the rack?" she asked politely.

Tessa stiffened as if she'd been struck. "It's from Topo's, actually," she choked out, naming an exclusive shop in downtown Branntville.

"Oh." Heather sighed. "I shop at Saks," she threw off, turning to Emma with a smile. "The band is delightful, isn't it?" she said, changing the subject deliberately. "Those dancers must be part of the floor show," she added, nodding toward the colorful group on stage.

"I hear the hotel's looking for a singer," Tessa said venomously. "Too bad your singing days are over."

The waiter arrived in time to save Tessa from having Heather's water glass emptied on her head. Cole glanced at her once, his eyes meeting hers levelly over the delicious platters of seafood, salad, and fresh fruit, and she felt her heart stop as she read the suppressed emotion there. She had to force her gaze back to her food.

The floor show was over by the time they finished eating. As they lingered over coffee and brandy the band swung into a slow, seductive number. Before Tessa could drop a hint to Cole that she'd like to dance, Heather saw her chance and took it.

"Dance with me?" she asked Cole, touching the lean, tanned hand lying on the table next to his coffee cup.

He stared at her, something like amusement in his silvery eyes. He stood up wordlessly, catching her slender, cool hand in his big, warm one, and led her out onto the dimly lit dance floor where five or six couples were making slow motions that resembled the two-step.

Cole caught her lightly around the waist and led her in a lazy fox-trot to the sweet rhythm, one eyebrow lifting in silent curiosity.

"Reckless little thing tonight, aren't you?" he mused. "Throwing verbal abuse at Tessa and dressing to the hilt. What are you up to?"

"Acting my age," she replied with a saucy smile.

"How much of it is acting?"

She dropped her eyes to his black tie. "I'm sorry about this afternoon." She hadn't meant to say that, but it slipped out.

"That we argued, or that you wore that miniscule bikini?" he asked in a deep, slow undertone.

She looked up at him, her eyes meeting his with the impact of silk against rock. "That...we argued," she murmured. The words were excess. They were talking with their eyes, with the slow, caressing movement of their bodies. Cole stroked her bare back with one hand while the fingers of the other locked tightly into hers.

"Closer, baby," he said quietly, urging her slender body nearer.

"Like this?" She looped her arms around his neck and pressed her body against his, shaking back her silky hair as she smiled at him.

"Yes, like that, you little witch," he murmured deeply, returning her smile. "How much have you had to drink?"

She blinked at him. "What makes you think I've had anything?"

"You're running toward me," he replied, his eyes searching hers in a silence that was sudden and complete. She felt his lean, strong hands caress her bare back with an overwhelming sensuality as he spoke.

"I'm a little afraid of you...like this," she admitted hesitantly.

"I know that. It's my own fault. I've given you reason to be." His hard face seemed to tauten with memory. He drew a deep breath and let his hands smooth her satiny skin down to her waist, bringing her body tightly against his so that she could feel every inch of him, warm and solid against her slenderness. She could feel his powerful legs brushing against hers when they moved, hear the soft rustle of fabric against fabric as his arms crossed behind her.

Her fingers tangled in the thick, cool hair at the nape of his neck, her long lashes lifting and falling shyly over the soft blue of her eyes.

"If you keep that up," he said in a deep, velvety tone, "I'm going to take you out of here."

Her hands stilled, and she held her breath. "And do what with me?" she whispered.

"My God, don't you know?" he asked in an urgent undertone. "Can't you feel what this is doing to me?"

Against her slender body, she could feel the hard, heavy throb of his heart, the harsh intake of his breath.

The realization that she could affect him that way was heady. Cole's self-control and cool nerves were almost legendary around the ranch, and she could make his heart run away with him!

She went on tiptoe against his tall, lean body, her lips poised just under his so that she could feel the smoky warmth of them. "It's...magic," she whispered shakily.

His hard fingers dug into her soft back. "Will you behave?" he growled harshly. "Heather, you're driving me out of my mind!"

"I'm getting even," she whispered against his hard mouth. "You've been driving me out of mine for days.... Oh, Cole, kiss me!"

His eyes flashed silver fire at her as he drew back with a jerky motion, his face rigid. "My God, you're brave in a crowd," he growled. "Hasn't anyone ever told you how suicidal it is to lead a man on like this?"

All her confidence oozed out in a sigh. Her hurt eyes dropped to his white shirt. "Chalk it up to moon madness," she murmured bitterly. "Maybe the strain of not being able to sing has snapped my mind. Just forget it, Cole."

"And that's the one thing I won't do," he ground out. The band stopped playing, and Cole moved away from her as if he'd been burned, grasping her roughly by the arm. He led her back to their table, but instead of seating her by Emma, he held on to her.

"Heather forgot her wrap and she's chilly," he said curtly. "I'm going to walk her back to the room to get it. We won't be gone long."

Emma looked from one rigid face to the other and smiled innocently. "Of course, dear, it isn't safe for a woman alone after dark in these deserted halls. We'll be fine until you get back."

"But, Cole . . ." Tessa called after them.

Cole, half-dragging Heather behind him, didn't even slow down. She felt her face burning with embarrassment and apprehension. She couldn't blame her brazen behavior on alcohol. She'd had hardly any. And judging by the rock hardness of Cole's face, she was about to catch the sharp edge of his tongue again.

"Cole, I'm sorry. . . ." she began as they reached the suite she shared with Emma.

He didn't answer her. He held out his lean hand for the key, his eyes frankly dangerous.

She reached in her bag and handed it to him with obvious reluctance. He opened the door, shepherded her inside, and closed and locked it behind him.

"Now," he said with a mocking smile, "would you like to repeat everything you said to me on the dance floor?"

She caught her breath, all her bravado and budding confidence as wilted as the flower in her hair. "Uh, no, I don't think so," she murmured, quickly turning away. "Would you like a drink?"

"I've had one, thanks."

"Cole, about what I said . . ." she began, stretching out a placating hand.

He moved away from the closed door, shedding his elegant jacket with lazy grace. His tie followed it into one of the upholstered chairs in the sitting room, and he flicked open the buttons of his white dress shirt with a careless hand, disclosing his bronzed hair-roughened chest as he walked toward her.

She backed away until the arm of the long, elegant blue-upholstered sofa was behind her knees. She caught her breath at the narrow, sensual smile on his dark face as he closed in on her.

"They'll miss us," she said in a voice so high pitched it sounded like someone else's.

"Not for a few minutes," he replied coolly. "Come here, Heather."

Her eyes fell to his bronzed chest, and she realized she wanted desperately to touch him. "Not like this," she pleaded. "Not to get even with me."

"Getting even is the last thing on my mind right now," he said quietly as he reached out for her. He drew her very gently against his long, hard body, and she smelled the clean, masculine scent of him, saw the strange flickering light in his pale eyes. The silence between them was tense with suppressed emotions.

"You've managed to get into my bloodstream," he told her. "I can't sleep anymore without dreaming about the taste of that soft, red mouth, the feel of your body against mine. My God, I walk around hungry, and you think you can tease me the way you have tonight and get away with it?"

Her breath was coming hard now. "I...I didn't think I affected you like that," she murmured.

"Like hell you didn't." He drew her closer, his arms riveting her to the length of him. "You knew what you were doing. You little witch, you were enjoying it."

"Weren't you?" she whispered softly.

"Oh, yes," he replied quietly. "Having you deliberately tempt me is enough to warrant a little enjoyment. But have you forgotten what I told you back at the ranch, Heather?"

She stared into his glittering eyes, all her bravado disappearing in a surge of apprehension. "What?"

"Something about...consequences?" he reminded her.

She drew in a deep breath, wondering how she was going to manage to talk above the sound of her own mad heartbeat. "Yes, Cole," she whispered. "I remember it very well."

His eyes flashed as he stared down into her flushed face with an intense scrutiny that made her breath catch in her throat.

"Were you trying to make me jealous this afternoon, with that Frenchman?" he asked softly, his voice deeply sensuous. "Did it bother you that I was paying more attention to Tessa than I was to you?"

It had bothered her, but she didn't want to admit it. "What makes you think that?" she murmured. Her eyes remained fixed on the broad expanse of chest revealed by his unbuttoned shirt.

"I'm a little old for games."

That brought her eyes up, as he'd known it would. When she met his fiery gaze, he bent, drawing her up on her tiptoes to meet his descending mouth.

She felt her body yield to his, her lips part in acceptance, and all the restraint went out of her. "Oh, Cole, it's been so long...!" she whispered hungrily, as his hard, warm lips came down on hers.

"Too long," he bit off against her soft, tremulous mouth. "Kiss me back, Heather."

It was like flying, she thought, like catching hold of a passing cloud and hitching a ride. Cole's mouth was devastatingly expert, his fingers half-soothing, half-arousing on her back where the low-cut dress left her shoulder blades bare under his rough hands. It was like the last time, only harder, slower, and there was a hunger in him that hadn't been quite so obvious that night in his study.

"My God, it took you long enough," he growled, lifting his head long enough to study her drowsy, half-closed eyes. "Relax, will you? You feel rigid."

"No, I don't," she whispered against his lips. Her hands went up to close around his neck. "I feel weak-kneed."

His nose rubbed against hers as he shifted his mouth to touch, lightly, the corner of hers in a soft, nibbling motion that made her turn her head and search for his warm lips. "What do you want?" he teased, his voice strangely soft, like brown velvet, his arms close, caressing.

"Kiss me," she whispered.

"Like this?" he murmured, brushing his lips lightly, tantalizingly, against hers.

"Oh, no," she whispered back, pressing closer. "Like this..." and she burrowed her soft lips into his, tempting him into violence, feeling his mouth open to hers, cling, possess as his hands slid down her body to catch her hips.

"Woman," he whispered roughly, his mouth poised just above hers, "you make my blood burn, you set my mind on fire. God knows I love kissing you, but in a minute kissing isn't going to be enough for me, do you know that? I'm not a boy anymore, Heather."

"I know that," she murmured, drawing her hands down to invade the soft fabric of his dress shirt. She slid her fingers under the edges to tangle in the mat of dark hair covering the bronzed muscles of his chest. "I've never known a man...who was...so much a man."

He kissed her roughly. "Are you listening to me?" he murmured.

She smiled against his mouth. "Not really. Why don't you kiss me again?"

He lifted her against him, his arms faintly bruising, the fabric of his shirt sliding against her bare arms as he held her a breath away from his mouth, his eyes almost on a level with hers. "You're making me hungry, Sunflower," he warned quietly. "Some men can take this kind of teasing, but I'm not one of them. I'm too hot-blooded."

She searched his darkening eyes, and everything she felt was in her glowing face. "I love you," she said softly. "Cole, I love you so much...."

Something wild flashed in his eyes. "We've always loved each other," he said noncommittally. "Since the beginning."

"Not like this," she murmured, leaning closer to brush her mouth tantalizingly over his, feeling the warm hardness of it as it parted involuntarily. "I love you...like this, Cole," she told him in a voice that wasn't quite steady. And then, daring everything, she kissed him with all the pent-up, aching hungers that had been gnawing at her ever since she looked at him and saw him as a man for the first time. Her arms held him, her mouth made promises, sweet promises that seemed to tear the control from him. All of a sudden, his arms were possessive, his mouth demanding, and time seemed to fade away while he kissed her, murmuring words she didn't hear, holding her trembling body against him, his hands tangling in her long hair to hold her mouth to his.

They were too lost in each other to notice the first knock at the door. It was several moments before the noise made any impression at all. Finally Cole drew away, his eyes almost frightening, his body as taut as a drawn cord.

"Yes?" he called, his voice sounding strangely unsteady.

"Cole, we're waiting for you; is anything wrong?" Tessa called back, her voice plainly impatient, irritated.

"We're just discussing business," Cole returned, and his tone dared Tessa to pursue it. "We'll be back in a minute."

"All right, darling, but do hurry, won't you?" Tessa called. A minute later they heard her footsteps pacing up and down the hall.

"She isn't going away," Heather murmured drowsily, still clinging to Cole.

"Obviously." He bent his head and nuzzled her mouth under his, and she felt the faint tremor in his hard-muscled arms. "I don't want to stop."

She smiled under his warm lips. "Neither do I. Let's stay here."

"You never did answer my question before," he murmured. "How much have you had to drink tonight?"

"Why, nothing," she protested, "except the wine I had with supper."

"Wine obviously goes to your head," he replied, looking down at her. "We'd better break it up. Tessa isn't going away."

When his arms left her, she felt strangely cold. He was eyeing her intently, his hair slightly mussed, his eyes silver fires. With his legs apart, his hands on his narrow hips, he was the picture of careless elegance.

"Are you coming back with me, or do you want to stay here?" he asked quietly.

"What do you want, Cole?" she asked, and her tone made it clear she was referring to more than the decision at hand.

He lifted his chin to look down at her. "I want you to tell me you love me, cold sober, in broad daylight, that's what I want."

She was too shocked to protest that she *did* love him, she always would. But before she could decide whether he was serious or just joking, Tessa's high-pitched voice shattered the silence again.

"Cole, the band will go home in a few minutes, and you haven't danced with me!" she wailed.

He muttered something unpleasant under his voice. "In a minute, damn it!" he called.

"You'd better go," Heather said gently. "I think I'll have an early night. I've had about all of Tessa I can take for one day."

He traced her mouth with a long, hard finger. "I haven't had all of you that I want," he whispered, bending to kiss her slowly, gently. "Not by a long shot. Spend the day with me tomorrow. A friend of mine has a beach house on the bay. He gave me the key before we came down here. We'll have breakfast on the arcade first, do some sightseeing, and wind up there for a swim."

Her eyes lit up. "Just the two of us?" she asked.

"My God, yes," he ground out, and she could see the flames leap up in his silver eyes as they searched hers. "I don't want an audience when we make love."

She flushed wildly, and hit him with her fist when she saw the mischief in his face. "You're a dreadful tease."

"At the moment, Sunflower, there isn't much else I can do," he told her, with a meaningful glance at the door. "Sure you won't come back with me? We could dance some more."

The temptation was terrible, but she shook her head, eyeing him covetously as he slid back into his evening jacket and tie and tidied himself in front of the mirror.

"All right, honey. I'll see you in the morning. The coffee shop opens at seven. I'll pick you up about five minutes before. Okay?"

She smiled at him, her whole heart in her eyes. "Okay. Good night."

He stared at her mouth and raised an eyebrow. "I'd give a lot to kiss you again, pretty woman, but I wouldn't bet on my chances of getting out the door if I did."

"Chicken," she taunted softly.

He threw her an amused look. "Dare me, honey, and see what happens, Tessa or no Tessa."

She lowered her eyes demurely. "I'll wait until tomorrow, I think."

"You do that." He winked at her before he opened the door, and she got just a glimpse of Tessa's white dress before it closed behind him. There was an outraged query, followed by a curt murmur, and then their footsteps faded away down the corridor. Heather did a wild, gay little dance around the room before she went to take her shower, her eyes full of new dreams.

Heather was just ready to fall into bed when Emma came in, her smooth face bemused, her eyes questioning.

"Something wrong?" Heather asked gently.

"It's Cole," came the musing reply. "I don't think I've ever seen him so edgy. He's like a purebred racehorse straining at the bit."

Heather tried to hide the smile that came over her face. "Why should he be straining at the bit?"

Emma shook her head, laying her purse down on the sofa. "I don't know. He came back from leaving you here, sat down, and promptly ordered a double Scotch. I left him a few minutes ago pacing up and down in his room." She sank down into the cushions. "He was muttering something about Tessa's bad timing!" She glanced at Heather's flushed face. "Have you been arguing with him again, my dear?"

The flush got worse. She shook her head, letting her eyes drop to the carpet.

"What happened?" Emma asked gently.

Heather licked her lips nervously. "I...I love him," she whispered, letting the words slip out. Her eyes darted apprehensively to Emma's as she waited for her reaction.

"Yes, I know," Emma said complacently. "You always have."

"Not...like this," was the strained reply.

Emma's gray eyebrows went up over dancing brown eyes. "So that's what was going on back here while Tessa fumed and smoldered at the table!"

Heather's face went dusky. "Well..."

Emma laughed delightedly. "Oh, darling, I'm not blind. I've seen this coming since the day you came home after the accident. He's hardly taken his eyes off you. Has he mentioned how he feels?"

"No." Heather turned away, looking out the window at the dark Caribbean. "I know he wants me. But I'm not at all sure of anything else."

"Cole's deep, child. I'm not sure he knows himself what he's feeling. He hates ties, you know. He always has."

"I know."

Emma sighed. "Heather, nothing would make me happier than to see the two of you married. But if it shouldn't work out..." She searched for words. "Cole can be impossible. I'd hate to see you completely dependent on him."

Heather turned, disappointed that Emma couldn't tell her everything would be all right.

Emma stood up, her eyes compassionate as she hugged the younger woman. "I wish I could reassure you," she murmured softly. "But with Cole I can't make any guarantees. He's his own man—always has been. If he loves you, he'll let you know all right. Just...don't lose hope."

Heather hugged her stepmother fiercely. "I love you so much," she said. "I can never tell you how much."

Emma closed her eyes, biting her lower lip as she returned the embrace. "Sweet little girl, I love you, too. You're the daughter I always wanted." She drew back and gazed fondly at the younger woman. "You'll be independent of Cole when I die, I've made sure of it. Whatever happens, you'll be provided for, even if you decide never to sing again."

Heather drew away, astonished, gaping at her. "What brought that on? What do you mean, when you die? You aren't sick?"

Emma laughed nervously. "Oh, no, of course not! I was just telling you that I've fixed things. Dying! My goodness, no, unless you can die of happiness! The very idea . . ." She took a little breath. "I don't know how domineering Cole might get if I weren't here to act as a buffer, that's all. I just wanted you to know that you'd be financially independent if anything happened, if I shouldn't be here to protect you."

Heather felt troubled. The words had an ominous sound to them. "Did that doctor you saw before we left say anything to you that you're not telling me?"

Emma turned away. "Now, what would he have said?" she asked in a strange tone. "Let's go to bed, darling; I'm so tired."

Heather started to pursue it, but Emma was already in the bathroom with the water running, and she gave up. In the morning they could talk. In the morning . . . she would see Cole again, and Heather could hardly wait for the night to end.

Chapter Six

Heather was already up and dressed when Cole came for her. She'd just taken time to peek in Emma's room, smiling in gentle amusement at the silvery head barely visible under the corner of the pillow. She wore a yellow patterned sundress over a modest white bikini, with low-heeled sandals. She had left her hair loose and it curled softly about her shoulders. The big blue eyes that looked back at her out of the mirror were still confused and excited from last night. To think of Cole wanting her like that made shivers race through her body. And the thought of a whole day with him was exhilarating.

He knocked on the door and she opened it quietly so as not to wake Emma. She noted with frank approval the attractive tan slacks and matching bush jacket he was wearing.

"Ready?" he asked, his voice pleasant, his eyes glittering with banked down fires as they wandered over her. "Got your swimsuit?"

"I'm wearing it under this," she told him. "Will I need my purse?"

"Not unless you're planning to skip town alone," he said dryly, standing aside to let her join him in the carpeted, dimly lit hall. "And you'll never get away from me now," he added, catching her fingers lightly in his as they headed for the elevator.

After breakfasting in the crowded coffee shop, they walked lazily along the street that ran parallel to the docks. The fishermen were readying their boats to go out, and masses of office workers jammed the sidewalks in colorful dresses and cool business suits. Cole drew her back against an old stone building where the sidewalk was cracked and faded with age, while two jitneys navigated the impossibly narrow little street in record time, daring pedestrians to leave their toes in the way.

Heather laughed delightedly, her eyes sparkling in the sunlight. "This is fun!" she burst out.

They wandered down the street where the smell of the sea was salty and the fragrance of fish came faintly to Heather's nostrils. Farther on, basket weavers were setting up for the day, their colorful hats, purses, dolls, and bags brightening the drab little street. "Two dollars," one of the vendors called to them, holding up a gaily patterned straw hat woven in greens and pinks. "Two dollars, and it's yours," she called in her musical West Indies accent.

Heather looked up at Cole pleadingly, and he reached for his wallet. Minutes later they were on their way again, with the jaunty little hat perched on Heather's silvery head.

"Wait until we get to Rawson Square," he told her. "That's where most of the vendors set up shop. And a lot of them stay on Prince George Wharf to catch the passengers off the cruise ships. Tourism is the number one business here," he added, nodding toward the three ocean liners in port. "Even banking is second to it."

"Do we have business interests here?" she asked curiously.

"Yes, we own a hefty percentage of a resort over on Paradise Island."

"Why aren't we staying there?" she asked.

He smiled at her. "Because I thought you'd enjoy this more. I like walking around the docks and going into the shops myself. Paradise Island is just a little more secluded, and exclusive."

"You funny millionaire, you," she chided gently, pressing her side against him affectionately. "You're just a cowboy at heart."

He laughed. "So I am. I haven't always had money, Sunflower," he reminded her. "I know what it is to scratch for a dollar."

"I don't," she admitted. "Unless you count trying to be a singer. That's not as easy as I expected."

"Let's not talk about that."

"But, Cole, I'm just as entitled to a career...."

"I said," he interrupted with a glittering glance, "let's not talk about it now."

She turned away, shrugging. That had hurt, but she wasn't going to admit it.

"Hey," he said, catching her hands in his roughly. "Don't go cold on me."

She glanced up at him and grimaced. "You're just unbearable sometimes, Cole."

He tapped her cheek with a long forefinger. "So are you. Come on, I'll show you the straw market."

They walked down the docks, all through the straw market, and into Rawson Square, where buyers could find everything from hats to tiny baskets, seashell art, colorful shirts, even wood-carvings. It was fascinating, and Heather, eavesdropping, loved the musical accents of the Bahamians, who seemed at once elegant, sophisticated, and completely at peace with themselves and the world around them.

A group of French sailors on leave went into one of the import shops just ahead of them, and Heather watched, amused, while they tried to pick up a couple of young German girls. Their efforts were almost pathetic, because the Germans spoke no French, and the sailors obviously spoke no German. After a few minutes of gesturing and laughing, the sailors nodded, waved, and left the shop to search for tourists who could understand them.

"Poor guys," Heather murmured.

Cole squeezed her hand and grinned. "Nassau's the best port on earth for young sailors," he told her.

"They'll find someone. There are plenty of French girls around, and even though they have strict mamas and papas, I suspect our sailor friends will get in a few soft words before they leave port."

"With all due respect, I think they had something more substantial in mind," she teased.

He only laughed, and pulled her out of the shop. They wandered all over Bay Street before they went back to get the rental car and drive around to Fort Charlotte. At the fort, they saw centuries old cannons and a dungeon with dummies on a very real rack. A guide with an ominous monotone of a voice related a hair-raising account of what had happened here when pirates invaded the island.

The outlying countryside was fascinating. The hibiscus was in full bloom, as were the bougainvillea and a dozen other subtropical species, including the famous poinciana tree with its flaming orange flowers. The roads were almost all paved, running along between palm trees and towering casuarina pines. Along some parts of the winding, narrow roads were stone fences, used by farmers to keep their cows from wandering. Heather drank in the heavenly scent of flowers and sea air, watching for occasional glimpses of the jewel-colored sea, her eyes seeking Cole's face while he talked about the history of the island.

All too soon, they'd toured the interesting spots, and the sun was already past its noon zenith. If only the day would never end, Heather thought wistfully, if only she could keep it in a bottle and never let it out.

* * *

Heather leaned back in the seat with a sigh and a smile. "Where to now?" she asked dreamily.

"My friend's house," he told her as he darted around a parked jitney and pulled into traffic. "I had a house down here several years ago, you know. I'm sorry now that I let it go. But I've been too damn busy these past few winters to do any traveling, and it was just sitting vacant."

She glanced at him, a slight frown on her lovely face. "You never took Emma with you," she mentioned absently.

He lifted an eyebrow, a corner of his chiseled mouth going up with it. "No, I didn't," he murmured.

She went fiery pink, shifting quickly in the seat to look out the window as the implication of his words struck her. "Oh," she said inadequately.

"I'm a man, Heather," he said gently. "And there's never been a reason not to have women."

She shook back her long hair. "I didn't say a word," she reminded him.

"You didn't have to." He slowed the car and pulled off onto an even narrower road. "Does it bother you that I've had women?"

"Yes," she admitted, without stopping to think.

"I'm glad," he said, reaching for her hand. His fingers curled around it warmly. "Because it bothers me like hell, thinking of other men touching you."

She stared down at the lean, brown hand holding hers, feeling the power in it, and her fingers linked with his. "No one ever has, Cole," she said gently.

"I've never felt that way about any man, except you."
Her eyes traced the hard lines of his face, meeting his
gaze for an instant before he turned the car into a long
driveway that led to a walled-in house on the beach.
"I...I wouldn't mind...if you touched me," she said
softly. "Or how."

His fingers gripped hers painfully. "My God, don't
say things like that when I'm driving, I'll wreck the
damned car," he growled.

She laughed softly. "How very flattering, Mr.
Everett," she said with a saucy glance.

"Remember what I told you back home, Heather?
You'd better be prepared to deal with the consequences when you flirt with me. Or have you already
forgotten what happened last night?"

"Nothing happened," she grumbled.

"By the skin of your teeth," he agreed tightly. "If
Tessa hadn't knocked on the door..."

"What were you going to do?" she teased.

His eyes met hers. "Make love to you," he said
quietly, watching the scarlet blush that belied her attempt at nonchalance.

She felt her heart going wild and she could hardly
catch her breath. "My, it's hot outside," she murmured in a strangled tone, fanning herself with a bro-
chure she found next to her on the seat.

Cole chuckled softly, watching her as he stopped in
front of the wrought-iron gate. "Giving up?" he
asked.

"You're out of my league," she admitted.

"You'll catch up." He got out and unlocked the tall gates. Minutes later he parked the car beside the house, a huge and lovely white stone structure with green shutters and a long front porch that seemed to go all the way around it. Beyond the house, which was surrounded by banana and mango trees, the beach stretched out with sea-grape trees growing gnarled and strangely beautiful along it.

"Gorgeous," Heather breathed, stepping out of the car to gaze at the beauty of the aqua crystal water.

"And there aren't any tourists," Cole mused.

He unlocked the door and Heather went into the cool, spacious guest bedroom to change. The white bikini was modest, but she still wished she'd brought a beach robe. It was too late now. She borrowed a white towel from the bathroom in the guest room and went outside to meet Cole on the beach.

It had been a long time since she'd seen him in bathing trunks. She wasn't prepared for the effect the sight of him had on her. He was leaning back against the trunk of a sea-grape tree smoking a cigarette, and she couldn't take her eyes off him. His broad chest was hair-matted, tapering down to a flat, muscular stomach and powerful, hair-covered legs. He had an athlete's body, one that would have drawn feminine eyes anywhere, and just looking at him made Heather go weak-kneed.

He turned, sensing the scrutiny, and his silver eyes narrowed as they ran down her slender body in the bikini. He bent to crush out his cigarette and moved toward her.

"The sun's hot," she said quickly to disguise her nervousness.

"You'll burn, baby," he said quietly. "Did you think to bring some tanning lotion?"

She shook her head. She couldn't hold his intense gaze, and dropped her eyes to his broad, bronzed chest.

"Hey," he said gently.

She let her eyes skim reluctantly up to his and saw a faint smile in them.

"I'm not going to do anything you don't want me to do," he told her, his voice deep and soft and slow. "So don't start tensing up on me. All right?"

She forced a smile to her lips. "It's so new...."

He touched her cheek lightly, and then her mouth, smiling down at her. "Swim with me," he said.

She let him take her hand and lead her into the swirling water. It was surprisingly warm and she could see the bottom. Stroking lazily through the water, she got lost in the sensation of swimming, of peace, of carefree enjoyment and gave herself up to the sea and the sun. When Cole suddenly surfaced beside her, Heather splashed water at him, watching a rare smile bare his even white teeth. It was a revelation to see him so relaxed, and she laughed at the teasing glint in his silver eyes as he sprayed the salty water back at her.

"Brute!" she accused, slinging her long, wet hair back from her eyes with a quick hand.

"Witch," he returned, and ducked his head to swim straight for her.

She squealed delightedly and tried to swim away, panicked, sunk, and felt his hands catch at her. She twisted away from him, laughing, too full of excitement and pleasure to notice that the jerking motion had loosened the ties of her bikini top. It wasn't until she made a forward dive that she felt the suit pull free as her body surged forward.

She stopped in the shoulder-deep water, gasping, watching the white halter top wash away toward the beach on a swelling wave.

"Just try to get away now," a gruff voice teased, and she felt Cole's hair-roughened arms catch her from behind. He had passed them around her waist to jerk her body back against him in the cool, soft water.

"Cole!" she burst out, trying to struggle free. As his forearms rode up a fraction, he immediately understood the reason for her outburst.

His hands moved abruptly down to her waist. "Where is it?" he asked, his amusement evident.

She sighed nervously, crossing her arms over her chest. "Halfway to Nassau, I imagine," she said with a jerky laugh.

"Stay here. I'll see if it washed up on the beach."

He swam away, leaving her worrying about what they'd do if he didn't find it. She couldn't possibly walk out of the water half-naked in front of Cole. And she had only the towel as a cover-up. Perhaps she could get him to bring it out and let her wrap it....

But that wouldn't be necessary after all, she noticed with a relieved smile. Cole was bending over, scooping up something dainty and white at the edge of the beach, and diving back into the water with it. Seconds later, a black head broke the surface beside her, and he pushed his hair back with a heavy sigh as he handed her the missing article.

"The authorities here are liberal," he remarked dryly, "but not that liberal."

She blushed, fumbling with the silly thing. She couldn't seem to get her fingers to work at all.

"Let me," he said gently, moving in front of her. "It's not the end of the world if I catch a glimpse of you."

His fingers, deft, confident, drew the top in place and he reached around her to fasten the ties in back. His eyes looked down into hers, searching, quiet, and his fingers suddenly stilled at her back. He didn't move. He seemed to have stopped breathing, and Heather could feel her own heartbeat shaking her as she met that steady, intense gaze.

"Heather . . ." he said quietly, bending.

She met him halfway, lifting her soft mouth to his.

His lips parted hers softly, gently, and there was nothing of passion in the kiss. Only a strange, new tenderness.

He drew away, meeting her confused gaze, the control he was exercising apparent in his taut features. The glittering silver of his eyes belied his composed expression. "Stand still," he murmured, making a knot in the ties at her back before he reached up to make another at her nape, his fingers cool and deft and steady as he secured the halter in place. "My God,

I've never kissed a woman like that," he said under his breath.

"Should I be flattered or insulted?" she murmured, her soft eyes openly flirting with his.

One eye narrowed as he looked down at her arrogantly. "How would you like me to untie these strings and start over again?"

She smiled, lost in the newness of being confident with him. "I'm not afraid of you."

"Said Red Riding Hood to the wolf," he murmured darkly.

"I know what *you* would have done if you'd been that wolf looking at Red Riding Hood from under the covers," she told him.

"I'll bet you do," he murmured back, one corner of his mouth lifting. "You'll take a lot of teaching, though, little Red."

"I could always get that Frenchman to help...." she suggested.

He caught her small waist and jerked her against him. "I'll teach you," he corrected, dropping a rough, hard kiss on her mouth.

"What will I need to know?" she asked in a breathless whisper.

His even white teeth nipped gently at the soft curve of her lower lip. "Not now," he whispered, smiling against the telltale trembling of her mouth. "It's broad daylight, and this is a pretty public place."

She met his dancing eyes. "And if it wasn't...broad daylight, and a pretty public place?"

He let her go. "Wait until tonight and I'll show you."

Her heart skipped a beat as she swam along beside him, barely able to keep pace with his long, graceful strokes. "Cole, are we having supper with Emma and Tessa?" she asked quietly.

"We're having it here, didn't I tell you?" He grinned at her stunned expression. "I've hired a caterer for the evening."

"Just for us?" she asked.

"For the two of us." He caught her hand and pulled her in to the beach with him, letting her sink down on a towel. He tossed her a smaller one to dry off with. "Were you in a hurry to get back?" he asked.

She smiled. "I thought you might be."

"Tessa doesn't have any claim on me, Heather," he said, all the humor gone out of his face. "Not one."

"You've spent a lot of time with her lately," she remarked, avoiding his piercing gaze.

"Yes, I have," he said noncommittally. He glanced sideways at her, his eyes laughing at the expression on her face. "Jealous?"

Her eyes met his and turned away toward the jeweled sparkle of the Caribbean. "Isn't it lovely here?" she asked in an enthusiastic tone.

"Lovely," he agreed, leaning back on his elbow. But he was watching Heather.

It was the most romantic supper Heather could ever remember. A table had been set up on the patio overlooking the Caribbean; the moonlight made silver shadows on her face; and the soft, warm breeze brushed against her bare arms and lifted her hair away from her shoulders.

Both of them were strangely silent, as if the tension she'd felt all day had transmitted itself somehow to Cole. He watched her quietly over the excellent Napoleon brandy he'd ordered as an after-dinner drink. His silver eyes glittered under the disheveled dark hair that fell over his brow, and he looked alarmingly masculine in a blue silk shirt that was open to the waistband of his white trousers. She had to drag her eyes away from him time and time again. She knew she'd remember this day with him, the magic of being alone with him, as long as she lived. As long as she loved him. Forever.

"You're very quiet," he remarked, his deep voice disturbing the quiet of the softly scented night.

She peeked at him over her brandy snifter and smiled shyly. "I'm enjoying the silence."

"So am I." He leaned back in the chair, resting his arm over the smooth mahogany back, and sighed. "God, I can't remember a time in my life when I needed a break so much. I'm glad you aren't one of those damned chattering females."

She smiled at him. "I thought you liked sophisticated, witty women."

He chuckled dryly. "They do have their uses," he agreed, his eyes twinkling at the blush that flamed on her cheeks.

"You are the most outrageous man..." she told him.

"Is the journalist outrageous?" he asked, narrow-eyed.

"Gil?" She smiled, shaking her head. "He likes to think he's something of a ladies' man, but he's really quite a shy, introverted person. He uses his smile like a shield."

He swirled the brandy in his glass. "You use your innocence the same way," he remarked quietly. "And it isn't necessary, not with me."

She chewed nervously at her lower lip and brushed a wisp of silvery hair away from her eyes. "I feel vulnerable with you," she admitted, clutching her glass with cool fingers as she let her eyes flicker up to his. "I've always been very cool with men up until now, I never got carried away. But when you touch me..." She flushed, shocked by her own admission.

"Don't be embarrassed," he said quietly. There was no mockery in his eyes now.

She caught her breath. "You used to be forever warning me about how dangerous men could be when they got excited," she reminded him. "So I've always been careful not to stir anyone up."

He laughed softly, both tender amusement and fierce possessiveness in his eyes. "Even me?" he probed.

"Especially you," she murmured, feeling the heat in her face. "I...I know how you are with a woman...now."

He studied the rim of his glass reflectively before his eyes went back to hers. "Do you like the way I am...with a woman?" he asked quietly.

Her pulse went wild. The glass trembled slightly in her hand and she put it down quickly. "I, uh, I think I'll go and watch the waves for a little while," she said evasively, "before we have to go back."

He stood up, too, and she knew without looking back that he was right behind her when she went down to the edge of the beach. She had left her shoes behind at the table, and she ran barefoot through the sand, playing tag with the soft, swirling foam of the sea.

He watched her quietly from the trunk of a sea-grape tree, smoking a cigarette, his eyes glittering as they took in the picture she made in her pale yellow dress, her hair flying, her skirts swirling as she danced along the damp sand in the moonlight. She was as beautiful as a fairy, as graceful as a ballerina. Perfect.

She went back to him laughing, her hair dancing on the sea breeze. She was exhilarated by the sea and the surf and the night and by being with Cole in the darkness. "Why don't you come, too?" she asked, laughing up at him. "You old stick in the mud, it's fun!"

He smiled patiently, his lean body the picture of elegance as he lounged lazily against the gnarled trunk of the tree. "When I finish my cigarette," he told her.

She stretched happily, winding her arms behind her head, her eyes closing as she savored the night. "I don't think I've ever enjoyed a day more."

"I know I haven't. And it isn't over yet," he added quietly.

She turned, meeting his eyes, and what she read in them froze her. She stood there in front of him in the silvery moonlight with her heart pounding madly. The verbal jousting they'd engaged in all day had been fun, but it was over, she read that in his face. He was ready to collect on all those teasing promises she'd been making, and quite suddenly all her bravado disappeared.

"Don't panic," he murmured as he threw down his cigarette and moved closer. "We'll go at your pace."

"It's...it's getting late," she burst out when he took her in his arms.

"Heather," he whispered gently, "I'm not going to force you."

She licked her dry lips and looked up at him helplessly, her fingers trembling where they rested on the silky fabric of his shirt. "I'm such a coward," she admitted with a nervous smile. "And I'm trying so hard not to be."

"Would it help if I let you make the first move?" he asked quietly.

She reached up and touched his very sensual mouth with her fingertips. Then she looked straight into his narrowed eyes. "How far do you want to go?" she asked in a whisper.

Some hint of violence flashed in his eyes and with a harsh, muffled curse he caught her waist and pushed her roughly away from him. He turned, ramming his hands into the pockets of his slacks, his profile brooding as he stared out to sea.

Heather watched him, puzzled, hurt by his sudden rejection. "Cole, what's wrong?" she asked hesitantly, reaching out a hand toward him, only to let it fall when his glittering eyes flicked toward her before he turned them back to the sparkling gleam of moonlight on the Caribbean.

He pulled another cigarette out of his shirt pocket and took his time lighting it. Then he took a deep, hard draw, the cigarette's tip glowing orange in the moonlit darkness. "What, exactly, do you think I want from you?" he asked, banked down fury in every soft word. "A passionate roll in the sand? What the hell makes you think I'd get anything out of making love to a very nervous virgin?"

She gaped at him. "You're making it sound sordid," she accused miserably.

"No. You are." He turned around and looked at her, his face like stone, anger in every tense line of it. "Asking me in that prim little voice how far I want to go...my God, I didn't bring you out here to seduce you!"

"Then...what do you want?" she faltered.

He sighed angrily before he turned away. "I don't know." His eyes narrowed on the sea. "God help me, I don't know." He shifted, flicking open the buttons of his shirt to let the breeze caress his bronzed torso. "I love my freedom."

She moved to stand beside him, her eyes watchful, wary. He looked immovable, with the moonlight shining on his dark hair, and she'd never loved him more. "I don't see the problem," she said quietly, forcing a smile to her mouth. "I haven't asked you to give up your freedom."

He laughed shortly. "You don't see the problem." He threw the cigarette into the surf and whirled, shooting out his lean hand to catch her waist and slam her body against his with a force that took her breath away. "Then let me show it to you, my dear," he ground out, his mouth crushing down on hers.

He had her off balance, and she had to hold on to his broad shoulders to keep from going over backwards. His mouth was angry, and he hurt her. She remembered her first encounter with him, the shock of his touch, and it was like reliving that kiss all over again. She could feel the tension in him, the pent-up desire that must find release. The only sounds in the sweet, lush darkness were the watery murmur of the surf and Cole's harsh breathing while he kissed her.

"Please," she whispered when he relented for an instant. "You're hurting..."

His breath came hard; his eyes were strangely dark. "I want you," he ground out, and his lean hands slid down her back to her hips, drawing her against his powerful legs until the warmth of his body seemed to burn against every trembling inch of hers. "Do you hear me, Heather?" he asked, his voice a husky growl. "I want you. That's the problem. Every day I come closer to doing something about it, and the day I do will be the end of everything for me."

She stared up at him helplessly. "But, you wouldn't..."

"Take you?" He smiled, but it wasn't pleasant. "Don't kid yourself. I told you at the beginning that I wasn't in my dotage. Hungry men get dangerous, honey, and I've never been this hungry in my life. Can't you understand? You're not safe with me anymore. You're not thirteen, and I'm not your brother. I'm a man, and this is what happens when I kiss you." He caught her hand and pressed it into the damp thicket of hair over his muscular chest, where the force of his heartbeat was making his hard body shudder. He bent and brushed his lips against hers with a teasing, tantalizing pressure that made her ache for something harder, deeper.

"Feel it," he whispered against her parted lips, moving her fingers against his cool chest. "Feel what you do to me. And you're so naïve, you don't even realize how you affect me."

But she did. And he was affecting her, as well. She was still shy of him, but the love inside her was a living, breathing thing and she wanted nothing more than to be held by him, kissed and touched by him, to forget everything but here and now and Cole. . . .

She slid her hands up his chest and around his neck, going on tiptoe against him, feeling the ripple that ran through him at her action. Before her courage could desert her, she touched her mouth to his, urging it closer, nuzzling into it until she felt him come to life. He was kissing her now, his mouth sensual, expert, thorough as it taught hers things she'd never known about kissing.

She felt his hand moving on her body, trespassing almost imperceptibly under the straps of the sundress, lightly tracing patterns on her back, her inner arms, her shoulders. "Cole," she whispered into his devouring mouth. "Cole, don't stop, please don't stop," she murmured dazedly, so lost in him that it would have been a torment to be put away from him now.

"Sea witch," he whispered huskily. He bent, lifting her completely in his arms to carry her a little way back up the beach and lay her gently down on the sand.

Her eyes opened drowsily and looked into his as his powerful body stretched itself alongside hers in the soft, powdery coral sand.

Her fingers touched him lightly, discovering the crisp hair on his bronzed chest, the steely hardness of his muscles, the slight roughness of his skin.

"Wait a minute," he whispered quietly, lifting himself just long enough to slide out of his shirt and toss it away. He eased back down alongside her, placing a forearm on either side of her to catch his weight. "Now touch me, Heather," he whispered again, his voice deep and slow and sensuous above her.

Her breath seemed to come with tremendous effort as she brushed her fingers over the powerful muscles in his upper arms and shoulders, feeling the cool flesh with a sense of awe.

"Enjoying yourself?" he asked quietly.

She looked up at him with a nervous smile, her hair spread around her like a wispy platinum fan, her eyes soft and drowsy. "You're very patient," she whispered. "And you don't feel patient, do you?"

He shook his dark head. "I want to do things to you that would shock you."

Her lips parted under a rush of breath. "Nothing you did to me...would shock me right now," she managed unsteadily. "I'm not afraid."

"I am," he said strangely. He bent and brushed his mouth across her lips. Then he trailed it down her throat to her smooth, soft shoulders where the square neckline of her sundress slashed across the slight swell of her small, high breasts. She caught her breath at the sensations it caused. His jaw was shadowed with a day's growth of beard, and its slight roughness was stimulating. She let her hands fall back over her head to rest in the cool sand, her eyes closed, her body arching to the slow, caressing lips that were tasting her silky skin.

His fingers eased under one of the straps that held the sundress in place and slowly, relentlessly, eased it down her arm. Her eyes flew open, looking straight up into his, half-frightened, half-hungry.

"I want to taste you like this," he whispered softly. "I want to see how it feels to run my lips over you."

Her heartbeat was frantic. She stared up at him in dazed silence, obviously vulnerable as his warm hand drew the strap down to her elbow and rested there. The cool breeze brushed against the soft bareness of her body like caressing fingers.

He let his gaze rest on her then, slow and bold, and his eyes narrowed slightly just before he bent his dark head. For the first time in her life she felt the intimacy of a man's lips on her soft body, and they were warm and faintly abrasive and utterly devastating.

"Cole...!" she gasped, a feeling of panic causing her to reach out and grasp his hair. Her hands clenched convulsively as his warm mouth made nonsense of her resistance.

"Don't fight me," he whispered against her silken skin. "Don't be afraid of me. Heather, my God, you're the most beautiful woman I've ever seen, ever touched," he murmured, a note in his voice she'd never heard before. "Sweet, sweet treasure, you taste of moonlight and sea spray, and white roses...." He lifted his head, his eyes meeting hers for just an instant before he moved. He let his chest lower down to rest very gently against her half-bare breasts, his mouth taking slow, sweet possession of her parted lips. His tongue lightly traced the inner softness of her mouth until she made a strange little sound, half-moan, half-gasp, and his hands slid under her body to lift her against him, holding her, protecting her, his ardor unlike anything she'd dreamed it would be. She'd expected a rough, hungry passion, but not this aching tenderness, this strangely protective quality that made her want to give him everything and heightened her love for him to such a degree it was almost pain.

A long time later he drew away and sat up, averting his gaze to the sea while he let the breeze lift his damp hair and cool his face. "Hand me a cigarette, sweetheart," he said in a voice that sounded unfamiliar and strained.

She had to fight to control her shattered emotions. Only a minute before she'd been drowning in his expert lovemaking, and now they might as well be an ocean apart.

With a little sigh she sat up, quickly tugging her bodice back in place with hands that trembled. She found his shirt and took a cigarette from the package in his pocket, handing it to him wordlessly.

He took it with steady fingers, his eyes returning to study her. As his gaze lingered on her disheveled hair and slightly swollen lips, on the faint marks on her shoulders, he smiled. "Embarrassed?" he asked gently when she quickly looked away.

She tried to smile, too, but her trembling lips wouldn't cooperate. She glanced at him and away, smoothing her unruly hair back from her flushed face.

He lit his cigarette and held it in one hand while he caught her fingers in the other hand. "That was a first for both of us," he said, his eyes patiently amused as they met hers. "Oh, yes, you young Puritan, I could tell it was the first time. You did everything but bite and kick to try to get away. Was it so hard to give in?" he asked quietly.

She felt the heat in her cheeks. "Inhibitions can be a little binding, you know."

"You'll get past yours." His fingers pressed hers lightly. "You did very well this time. Those sharp little nails were making scratches down my back just before I let you go."

She laughed softly, flushing at the memory of how tightly she'd been clinging at the last. "You make my head swim," she admitted softly.

"You make mine swim, too, honey." He took a long draw from the cigarette. "You've dated men since you left home, haven't you?"

"Yes," she admitted.

"You must have found some of them attractive," he persisted.

She shrugged. "Some."

"And yet this was the first time you'd ever been touched," he added, his eyes faintly curious. "Weren't you ever curious enough to experiment, honey?"

She couldn't hide the smile or the amusement that sparkled in her blue eyes. "Yes," she said, "but you never took me seriously before."

He stared at her. "Do I take that to mean that you've never wanted to experiment with any man but me?"

"Can I help it that you're so sexy you leave other men in the shade?" she murmured, flirting outrageously with her eyes.

Both his dark brows arched, and a strange expression came into the silvery eyes under them. "Sexy, am I?" he murmured, taking a final draw from the cigarette and then tossing it into the surf.

She laughed excitedly and tried to tug her fingers away from his possessive grip. "Yes," she giggled. "Let go."

"No. Come back here."

"Let go!" She struggled, laughing, and suddenly found herself flat on her back with the weight of his powerful body pinning her to the ground.

"Coward," he challenged, staring down at her with laughter glittering in his eyes.

"You bet," she laughed back. She sighed, linking her arms around his neck, and staring up at him with all the old fears gone. Only her pleasure in being close to him was left. "Oh, Cole, I'll never forget today. Not a second of it."

"Neither will I." He bent and kissed her softly, slowly. "We'd better go back to the hotel. I want you very much, Miss Shaw."

"Am I in terrible danger?" she asked impishly.

"You could be."

"Promises, promises," she whispered, raising herself just far enough to kiss him lightly on the lips.

He smiled down at the picture she made. "Moonlight suits you, Sunflower," he told her. "You look like a fairy lying there."

"I'm not surprised," she murmured. "It's been a magical night."

"Yes," he agreed, kissing her once more, gently, before he sat up. "Bedtime for you. It must be going on midnight by now."

She looked into his eyes, and had the strangest feeling of impermanence, as if this dreamlike moment might fade away, leaving her with the nightmare of life without Cole. "Cole!" she whispered shakily.

"Hey, what is it?" he asked, when she threw herself against him and clung as if she were frightened. "Honey, what is it?"

She buried her face in his warm throat. "Hold me for a minute," she whispered, "just for another minute. Hold me very tight, Cole." Her voice broke as she felt his big arms contract around her, crushing her to him. The contact was soothing, protective, and in a minute she'd forgotten the twinge of fear that had overcome her. She drew back, a little embarrassed at her emotional display. "Sorry," she murmured. "I don't know why I felt that way."

"It's been an exciting night," he murmured with a wry glance. "Come on, fairy, let's round up our unicorns and go back to the castle."

She laughed up at him, all her new confidence shining out of her eyes. This was just the beginning, she thought dazedly as she walked beside him, holding tight to his lean fingers. There was plenty of time to explore the new relationship they'd found tonight. All the time in the world.

Chapter Seven

Cole parked the rental car in the lot and walked Heather toward the front of the hotel, his arm possessive around her waist. Neither of them paid any attention to the small group of French sailors on their way back to the docks or to the strolling couples enjoying the cool night air.

"We'll do this again tomorrow," he said as they passed a departing German couple and started up the steps where the doorman was standing.

She smiled up at him, dreams filling her eyes. "Oh, could we, Cole?" she asked softly.

He stopped, staring down at her, his silver eyes glittering wildly. "Oh, God, I wish we were alone," he growled under his breath. "I'd kiss the breath out of you!"

Her lips parted involuntarily, and her eyes yielded to his.

"We'd better get inside before I lose what little mind you've left me," he said in a half-humorous tone.

She smiled secretly, nodding and saying good-night to the friendly doorman with what she hoped was a steady voice.

As they entered the lobby Tessa stirred on the long sofa just past the mirrors, stretching lazily in her dressy white pantsuit. "So there you are, finally," she murmured, her eyes focusing on Heather, missing nothing as they studied the disheveled hair, the swollen mouth, the light in her soft blue eyes. Heather was sure the other woman felt murderous, but nothing showed in the smiling face she turned to Cole.

"How about a nightcap, darling?" she asked him pleadingly. "There's something I just have to talk with you about."

"Don't mind me." Heather yawned. "All I want is a quick bath and bed. I'm very tired," she added with a smile that was for Cole alone.

He returned it, his eyes unusually tender. "Good night, baby," he murmured. "Pleasant dreams."

"You, too." She turned. "Good night, Tessa," she added as an afterthought.

Tessa, already leading the way to the hotel bar, didn't even bother to answer her. She latched on to Cole's arm possessively, noting with secret anger the sand on his silky shirt. She'd already noticed identical evidence on Heather's dress, and she only hoped there was still time to divert Cole from his obvious goal. She didn't need a videotape to know what had been going on between Cole and Heather, and she intended to stop it dead—right now.

She sat down at the glass-top table with Cole and smiled up at him as he ordered a couple of tall piña coladas. "Ummmm, delicious," she murmured when the waiter had brought their drinks. "Fresh coconut and pineapple juice. It never tastes like this at home, does it?"

Cole sipped his own drink. "All right, let's have it," he said without preamble. "What's on your mind?"

Tessa stared into her frosty glass and was quiet for a minute, marshalling her thoughts. This had to be done just right or Cole would get suspicious, and that would never do. "You and Heather are getting pretty thick, aren't you?" she finally asked.

Cole stiffened. "Is that any business of yours?"

His voice chilled her blood and she looked up, braving his glittering eyes. "I think it might be, since I know something you don't know."

He leaned back in his chair, looking so impossibly attractive that she ached to be able to touch him, hold him. She'd never wanted anything but Cole in all her life. "What could you possibly know that I don't?" he asked lazily.

"I was with Deidre Shaw when she died," she reminded him. "We were very close, remember?"

His eyes narrowed. "I remember. So?"

She watched the ice in her glass as she stirred the milky drink. "You know how she admired your father?"

"Who didn't?" He scowled, bitterly remembering the woman's obvious flirtatiousness. He'd never cared for Heather's mother.

"She was very beautiful when she was younger, and there was some sort of accident on the ranch while Jed Shaw was away from home." She peeked at him to make sure she had his attention before she plunged ahead. "She needed help and Big Jace was just a few miles away. He got out of bed in the middle of the night to go help his best friend's wife." She sighed. "To make a long story short, Deidre tempted him one time too many. Nine months later, Heather was born."

He stared at her. He didn't say a word, but his big hand tensed and the glass shattered in his fingers, drenching the table. He seemed unaware of what he had just done. Their waiter had disappeared and the bar was deserted now except for the two of them and the sleepy bartender. "What did you say?" he ground out.

"Deidre never told anyone else," Tessa said with her voice lowered. "It would have destroyed your mother, and Deidre knew it. But she loved your father so much...and at the last, she just...blurted it out. I've never told another soul. But when I saw what was happening between you and Heather...well, I just had to tell you before you made a tragic mistake. You do realize what I'm saying?"

His eyes were terrible, and if Tessa had had any doubts about what he was beginning to feel for Heather, they were swept away by the agony in his face. For an instant she almost regretted the lie. But it was too late to turn back now. "Heather is your half-sister, Cole," she added, driving the knife deeper.

He just sat there, his face white under its tan, his jaw taut with shock and fury. "If you're lying to me, I'll make you rue the day you were born," he said in a voice that left no doubt he would carry out his threat.

For just an instant she gave in to a horrible fear that she might be found out some day in the distant future. But it was only a fleeting regret, quickly gone. She shook her head. "I'm not lying, I swear. Cole, you know yourself how Deidre was always clinging to your father," she said. "You know it."

He did know, but he'd never noticed any response on his father's part. Of course, Big Jace had been a private person, tight-lipped....

"I'm so sorry," Tessa murmured gently, playing the part to the hilt. "I had to tell you, you do understand that, don't you?"

He stared at the shards of glass on the table and the milky puddle of piña colada, his eyes blank.

"Cole?" she whispered.

"Go and get me another drink," he said in a voice like steel.

She got up, pausing to lay a compassionate hand on his big shoulder. He shook it off, his jaw set, his body rigid. She went to the bar and got the drink for him, faint misgivings clinging to her like cobwebs. He'd get over it. She'd see to that.

She took the piña colada back and used a few napkins to clean up the mess. "Here, this will make you feel better," she promised.

He took two huge swallows of it, his eyes glittering at her. "My father may have had one hell of a night with Deidre Shaw," he said quietly, "but being the man he was, he'd have told Emma about it at some point in his life. That's the way he was. If what you say is true, all I have to do to confirm it is to ask her. And that's where I'm going right now." He gulped down the rest of the drink and stood up.

"But...she might not have known!" Tessa burst out.

"She would have known." He studied her through narrowed eyes. "Before I ask her, do you have anything else to say?"

Tessa stood her ground. There was a chance that Big Jace wouldn't have told Emma, and Cole knew it. Tessa wasn't backing down an inch. She'd placed the doubt in his mind and she was going to leave it there come hell or high water. At least this way she still had one last chance to get him to the altar. "I don't have anything else to say," Tessa replied coolly.

He turned without another word and left the bar.

"Oh, my God!" Heather was staring down in anguished shock at the lifeless body burrowed under the covers. Putting her hands over her mouth, she tried desperately not to panic.

She had taken a shower and was just on her way to bed when she decided to check on Emma. The older woman was lying in bed in the same position she'd been in when Heather left the room that morning. She was fine then; Heather had seen her chest rising and falling. But sometime between morning and midnight, something had gone terribly wrong, and there hadn't been a soul around to help.

With a gasp of pure horror, she ran for the telephone just as the knock came at the door to their suite. She fumbled with the knob and threw open the door, her eyes wild, her heart pounding frantically. It was Cole standing there, looking as grim as she'd ever seen him.

"I need to talk to my mother," he began before Heather could speak.

"Cole, come quickly," she whispered frantically, tugging at his arm. "Oh, please, it's... it's Emma!"

His heart seemed to stop when she dragged him into Emma's room. He knew immediately. He'd learned to recognize the look of death instantly in Vietnam; he knew the posture of it from long experience. But this was no enemy soldier on the battlefield; this was his mother. "I'll get the doctor," he said tersely. He paused just long enough to brush the wild hair away from Heather's face, to make sure she was all right, even though his heart felt as if it was going to break. "Go and wait in the sitting room, honey," he said softly. "Go on, there's nothing more you can do."

"Aren't you going to... to check?" she whispered, her eyes so wild and full of terror he wanted to crush her against his body and protect her from all of it. But he couldn't.

"There's no need," he said in a voice so solemn she knew better than to argue.

She only nodded and went out of the room in a daze, the tears just beginning to come to her eyes.

The next few minutes were a nightmare. Heather could hardly believe it was happening. The night before, she and Emma had been talking so comfortably, and now Emma was dead. If only she'd checked on the older woman, if only...!

Cole waited with her outside the bedroom while the doctor made his examination and wrote out the death certificate. His face was a mask of grief.

"Are you all right?" she asked when the doctor had gone.

He nodded. He was standing by the window with his hands in his pockets, so alone that the sight of him touched Heather.

"Can I get you something, a cup of coffee, a drink?"

"Nothing." He ran a careless hand through his hair. "I'll have to make arrangements for getting us home. I'd better go and take care of that right now. Will you be all right?" he asked kindly, turning to study her drawn face.

"I'll be all right, Cole," she managed despite the tears that threatened to choke her voice. Just the sight of the closed door to Emma's bedroom was enough to set her off again. She couldn't bear it. "Oh, Cole, I shouldn't have left her; I should have checked...!"

He moved across the room and took her in his arms, his touch strangely impersonal but tender, so different from the way he'd held her earlier. "Heather, it was quick. I promise you, it was quick. And nothing you could have done, even if you'd been with her, would have stopped it. Nothing would have helped. I asked the doctor. It was a massive coronary. Let's just be grateful that she didn't suffer, and not dwell on regrets."

She nodded, wiping her tears with the back of her slender hands. She looked up at him like a lost child. "What do you want me to do?"

"Stay here until I get back. All right?"

Heather nodded. She curled up in one of the easy chairs while the tears rolled silently down her cheeks. She didn't watch him go out the door.

They left for home after a sleepless night.

Tessa had been a greater trial than the unpleasantness of moving Emma from the room to the hospital to the airport. She clung to Cole like flypaper, all tears and wild eyes and hysteria, her long red nails biting into the fabric of his jacket, even while he was doing his best to comfort Heather, who was far more heartbroken than Tessa.

"I loved her so," Tessa wailed on the way to the airport. Heather stared out the window at the beautiful aqua water, the white coral beach and sea-grape trees, without really seeing them.

"We all did," Cole said.

"You don't know how much I loved her," Tessa mumbled into her handkerchief. "She was so good, such a lady. I'd have done anything for her, anything."

Heather leaned her head against the seat and closed her eyes. If only Tessa would shut up. How horrible to pretend that kind of grief, and it *was* pretense, she knew it. Every minute or so Tessa would peek at Cole's averted face to make sure he knew how distraught she was. Any woman would have seen through her. But Cole was grieving too, and despite the fact that he wouldn't allow anyone to comfort him, he took Tessa's display at face value. Heather simply endured it with as much grace as possible. Emma would have wanted that, she reminded herself. Emma was never deliberately unkind to anyone, not even to Tessa, despite the provocation she'd given over the years. Tessa had never been anything but condescending with Cole's mother, and Heather knew it even if he didn't.

By late afternoon they were home. Heather got out of the black Lincoln with a sense of unreality. She stared blankly at the house, tears rushing to her eyes as she remembered leaving it only three short days ago. Then Emma had been alive and laughing. Now, her stepmother would never run onto the porch to meet her again, never wander through the gardens or complain about the insects that attacked her roses every spring.

"Don't," Cole said quietly. He put his arm around her and drew her close to his side. Heather was glad they'd already dropped Tessa off at her home, because her determined rival would surely have found some way to deny her even this little bit of comfort.

"I miss her so," she admitted, looking up at him with the grief plain in her eyes. "I know you do, too, even though it doesn't show. You hurt inside."

His long fingers tensed. "You know me pretty well, don't you?"

She nodded. "As much as you let anyone know you," she agreed. "You're a very private person."

He turned her toward the house. "Let's get Mrs. Jones to fix us some dinner, and then we'll work out the funeral arrangements. You'll have to decide about the flowers. I can handle the pallbearers and the rest of it."

She pressed still closer to him. "Roses, Cole," she murmured tearfully. "She loved roses."

The small Baptist church was crowded, and the smell of flowers was almost overpowering. Heather sat beside Cole in the front pew, just a few feet from the mahogany casket. She heard the faint strains of "Amazing Grace" echoing from the church organ that Emma had bought for the congregation last year. The familiar hymn brought her to tears. It had been Emma's favorite, a simple but eloquent tune, sweet and sad. Her hand searched for Cole's big one and she linked her fingers in his. He stiffened for just an instant before his hand relaxed and he allowed their fingers to entwine.

She didn't question the hesitation. Cole had been distant with her since Emma's death, but Heather thought she understood. He'd loved his mother fiercely, and Cole wasn't a man to seek comfort or sympathy. He was more like a wolf, who, when wounded, sought only solitude. He kept every hurt deep inside himself. No emotion showed on his hard face.

She glanced at him, her own pain in her eyes. She would have given anything to have spared him this, to have taken the hurt on herself completely. This was love, she thought, in its purest sense—sharing grief and trouble as well as the good times. Her fingers tightened gently and he looked down at her. For an instant she saw the torment he was feeling; then his eyes narrowed to conceal it.

"I loved her, too," she whispered softly.

He swallowed, returning the pressure of her hand. "I know."

Around them the buzz of conversation ceased as the last faint strains of "Amazing Grace" faded, and the minister stood before the congregation, his voice quiet and caring as he began the funeral service with a story about Emma—and a family that benefited from one of her numerous anonymous acts of generosity.

Heather listened, but her eyes were on the smooth mahogany of the casket. How mortal we are, she thought, how very mortal, and how suddenly our lives can be extinguished. If it had been Cole lying there instead of Emma... Her eyes closed and she gave thanks with every breath in her that Cole was alive and strong and healthy. She was grateful that she too was alive to hold his hand, to sit close beside him, to love him.

Emma had been a deeply religious woman, the minister was saying, her home in the hereafter was assured, and someday the congregation would join with her again in a world where there would be no sickness, no death. The organ began to play. The choir sang. The congregation stood and filed out to the cemetery. Heather clung to Cole's hand while the minister murmured something about ashes to ashes and dust to dust. There was a prayer. It was over.

Time seemed to hang suspended after the funeral. Cole threw himself into ranch work and business as if there was nothing else in his life. He was forever away for financial reasons—attending meetings, discussing mergers, inspecting potential additions to the herd, purchasing, selling, planning. New buildings were going up on the ranch; machinery was being replaced. Soon it would be spring—time to plant crops and cull the herd and build the empire even bigger than it was.

Bob Andrews, the family attorney, appeared shortly after the funeral to read Emma's will. Notoriously forgetful and almost disheveled in appearance, he looked strangely out of place behind Cole's scrupulously neat desk. He fumbled with the will and had to pause to search for his glasses—which he finally found under an envelope on the desk itself.

There were no surprises. The ranch and properties were equally divided between Cole and Heather, but there was a rider stating that Cole was to have absolute authority in business matters and that neither of them could sell property without consulting the other.

Heather sat through it dry-eyed, hardly hearing Andrews' pleasant voice. The inheritance meant nothing without Emma. All she wanted now was to get it over with, so she could begin to forget the sorrow and grief.

Cole's eyes were unreadable. He listened until the reading was over, nodded his head curtly, and left the room without even looking at Heather. Hurt, she could no longer excuse his manner by telling herself it was caused by grief for his mother. His rejection of her was becoming obvious and she fancied everyone noticed it. Even Mrs. Jones, who pretended not to notice anything, gave Heather strange looks at mealtimes. Cole was rarely present at the table anymore. It seemed he always had avalanches of business to attend to from morning till night.

"I'm not hungry," Cole growled. It was a week after the funeral, and once again he had found some excuse to skip dinner. With frank distaste, he eyed the plate of sandwiches and the fresh cup of steaming black coffee that Mrs. Jones had set in front of him.

"You can't work if you starve yourself to death," she scolded.

His face went rigid, but he didn't say a word. He picked up the coffee cup and sipped, his eyes blankly staring at the mass of paperwork in front of him.

"Mr. Cole, is something wrong?" Mrs. Jones asked suddenly.

He glanced at her. "No." He took another sip of the coffee and eyed her sharply. "I want to ask you something. Before my father died, when the families used to get together, did you ever notice anything going on that shouldn't have been?"

She started to speak, stopped, and sighed heavily. "Well, yes, I did, but it wasn't my place to say anything," she reminded him. "And it was nothing Mr. Jace could help, if you know what I mean."

He did, and it cut him to the quick. As he had feared, the housekeeper's words substantiated what Tessa had told him. His father had been a hot-blooded man—perhaps he *couldn't* help being attracted to Heather's mother.

"Thank you," he said quietly. "I just wanted a second opinion. Thanks for the sandwiches, too. I'll give them a try, fair enough?" He smiled, but there was no warmth in his eyes. They were like gray ice.

"No trouble at all. If you want more, just holler." She turned and went out. Poor Mr. Cole. It must have been hard on everybody, the way Deidre Shaw had flirted so outrageously with his father. She could have told him about the night she'd heard them arguing, when Deidre had invited Big Jace into her bed and he'd threatened to tell her husband if she didn't stay away from him. There'd been more, too. She could still see those icy gray eyes flashing, the way Mr. Cole's did when he lost his temper. And Big Jace calling Deidre Shaw everything but a lady while he told her that he was in love with his wife, that he didn't have affairs, and that Deidre would do better to pay some attention to her own poor, neglected husband instead of flirting with him.

Mrs. Jones sighed, shaking her gray head. She could have told Mr. Cole all that, but she was sure he'd heard about it. Mr. Jace had probably raised quite a ruckus at home telling his wife about what had happened. She reached up to the cabinet and took down her sifter. She'd bake Mr. Cole a chocolate cake. He loved them, and a nice cake would be sure to whet his appetite.

The following day, Heather realized she could bear no more of Cole's distant manner. She had to know what had happened to change his attitude toward her so drastically. Although she was nervous around Cole as she'd never been before, she gathered up the courage to go and ask him what was the matter.

He was leaning back in the oak chair behind his massive desk, his eyes cold and narrow, his body strangely taut as she reached the door and waited.

"Well?" he asked curtly.

"I'd like to talk to you, if you have time," she said, fighting down the urge to back away from him. This cold stranger wasn't the man she remembered from Nassau.

"I don't, but go ahead," he said, pausing to light a cigarette. "What's on your mind?"

She perched nervously on the very edge of the long red leather couch, her hands sedately folded in the lap of her creamy beige knit dress. "I'd like to know why you stare holes through me lately," she said with a pitiful attempt at lightness, her eyes more solemn and plaintive than she knew. "What have I done to make you so distant?"

He stared at a pencil on his desk, as if he'd never seen one before, the forgotten cigarette sending up curls of smoke. Under the bright light of the crystal fixture, his dark hair gleamed like jet, falling roguishly over his jutting brow as if his fingers had worried it. "Am I distant?" he asked absently.

"Cole, you can't have forgotten...?" she burst out, her heart in her pale blue eyes.

He got up with a strangely jerky motion and, retrieving his cigarette from the ashtray, moved to stare out the darkened window. "A lot has happened since we left for the Bahamas," he said quietly.

"I know." She stood up and moved behind him, her eyes lingering on his dark hair, the broad, powerful set of his shoulders under the burgundy velour shirt he wore. She touched his back lightly, surprised when the action made him stiffen.

"Heather, we've got to talk," he began, his face taut and drawn when he turned suddenly.

She smiled up at him, her heart in her eyes. "I know what it is," she murmured. She moved close, her eyes worshiping as she fixed them on his dark face. "You told me that night that what you wanted most was to hear me say that I loved you, cold sober, in broad daylight.''

''Heather . . . !'' he ground out.

She pressed close against his rigid body, her arms lifting to clasp around his neck, her emotions like flames burning in her soft blue eyes. ''It isn't broad daylight,'' she admitted, ''but I've never been more sober than this in my life. Oh, Cole, I do love you so! I love you, I love you . . . !''

With a strange, harsh sound, he tore her arms from his neck and pushed her away. His silver eyes blazed down at her from his lofty height.

''I can't . . . I don't love you . . . that way,'' he said, the words torn from him. ''I'm sorry.''

She stared at him, the words only beginning to penetrate her befuddled mind. He didn't love her. *He didn't love her.* ''But we . . .'' she began, her voice strained, uncertain.

He turned away to crush the cigarette out in the ashtray on his desk. ''I let things get out of hand in Nassau,'' he said curtly. ''You went to my head. I realize now that you took it seriously. But I never meant for that to happen. I thought you understood that it was just a pleasant diversion, Heather.'' He laughed shortly and turned away so that she missed the expression on his face. ''I should have remembered how naïve you are.''

She felt as if she'd been stabbed. All those warm, tender, passionate kisses he'd given her, the joy of being with him—she could have sworn he was as deeply in love as she was. But it had all been a sham. Something to pass the time. A diversion. She'd bared her heart to him, blurted out her love, and he was throwing it back in her face, laughing at her....

It took every ounce of willpower in her to face him. She straightened, gathering the torn edges of her pride together.

"I see," she said in a ghost of her normal voice. "I'm . . . sorry, I didn't realize. . . . You have to allow for my age, Cole," she managed with a faint laugh. "I'm just learning that men don't have the same ideas about commitment that women do. I'd forgotten . . . how much you love your freedom. You did warn me, that night on the beach. . . ."

His eyes flashed wildly, but she couldn't see his expression through the tears gathered in her eyes. "When are you going back to Houston?" he asked curtly.

"As soon as possible," she said without thinking. She turned and started toward the door, pausing with her hand on the doorknob to glance back at his rigid face.

"I'm sorry if I embarrassed you, Cole," she said in a tremulous voice. "It won't happen again."

He stared back at her, and there was something in his eyes that held her gaze even against her will. For just an instant she had the wild impression that he was hurting every bit as much as she was, maybe even more.

She turned and went out the door, closing it very gently behind her. As she went blindly up the stairs she imagined she heard her name groaned as if by someone in unholy torment. But it could only have been her imagination.

Chapter Eight

The next day she carefully locked the door behind her and went to the piano, her heart pounding nervously. She had told Cole she was going back to Houston, and she meant to keep her word. Her share of Big Spur was tied up in bonds and operating capital, and there wouldn't be more than a small allowance each month until she reached her twenty-first birthday in the summer. Now that she planned to leave Big Spur, she had to have money. And the only way she could possibly earn it would be to go back to her career—whether she wanted to or not. She hadn't even hummed since the accident. She didn't know if she had the strength to go back to the life she'd led before the accident. But she was going to give it her best shot. It was her only way out of an intolerable situation.

She pulled out the piano bench and sat down, easing back the silky wood cover to expose the spotless black and white keys. She touched middle C experimentally, and then let her fingers stretch out to a chord. The piano was in perfect tune.

Bits and pieces of a song she'd been working on in her mind for months began to fall into place under her graceful fingers. She closed her eyes and let the music transport her away from her grief.

She played the introduction and then let her voice take up the slow, seductive melody. "Sad, sad eyes, melancholy eyes," she sang, "tears are raining from your lovely eyes...how many dreams have found their rainbow's end in you...how many nightmares have those teardrops beckoned to...sad, sad eyes, melancholy eyes, how dark the shadow of your dying love...memory and melancholy can't warm the ashes of...the melancholy love that hides...behind the sadness of your sad, sad eyes...."

The tune whispered away under her sultry voice, and she knew the song had potential. It was just as the doctors had told her—there was nothing wrong with her voice. Her inability to talk after the accident had been caused by shock alone. She realized suddenly that her reluctance to try her voice had come more from her doubts about continuing her career than any real fear that her vocal cords had been damaged. Now all she had to do was find someone else to believe in her. Someone...Gil!

She ran to the phone and dialed the newspaper office. As lucky as the Irish, she thought when he picked up the line as soon as the switchboard buzzed him.

"Hi!" She laughed, pretending a gaiety she couldn't really feel. "Guess who?"

"An angel, as I live and breathe!" He chuckled. "How are you, blue eyes? You sound great! When are you coming back to me, or is the evil stepbrother still holding you prisoner?"

She felt her heart crack, as it had last night when Cole had put an end to her dreams. Her eyes closed and opened, and she drew a steadying breath. "I want to come back. Know any bands who need a vocalist?"

"Funny damn thing," he said. "I do. They're a soft-rock group: three guitars and a set of drums. Nothing bluesy. Think you might cope?"

"I'd like to try. Are they auditioning now?"

"Sure!" She knew he was grinning, even long-distance. "I'll tell them they are. How about tomorrow night?"

She swallowed, clutching the phone cord. "So soon?"

"The sooner, the better, as far as I'm concerned," he said, serious now. "I've missed you something terrible."

"I'll catch the first available flight out tomorrow."

"Fantastic!" he exclaimed enthusiastically. "By the way, I know the A and R guys at two of the biggest record companies in the state. If things work out with this new band, maybe I could talk to them...."

She laughed quietly. "I can see my troubles will be over if I stick with you, Gil. Thanks. You're a real friend."

"It's the least I can do," he said softly. "So long. Call me from the airport and I'll come get you." He hung up.

The following afternoon Heather dressed in a warm aqua knit skirt and top with matching shoes for travel. Her bags were packed, her face perfectly made up to disguise the traces of tears, her hair wound into an elegant French knot at the back of her head. She searched in her closet for the old handbag in which she kept her papers and money. As she did so her eyes were drawn involuntarily to the silky fur coat Cole had given her, her good-luck charm. She closed the closet door on it and turned away. She'd freeze before she'd ever wear it again.

She took her suitcase downstairs and called one of the ranch hands away from the stables to take her into Victoria where she would catch a plane to Houston. But when she brought her bag out to the truck she found Cole striding toward her, dressed in a dark gray business suit with a conservative tie, the very image of a successful tycoon.

Heather hadn't seen him since their confrontation in his study the night before last. It was as if they'd both made an effort to keep out of each other's way. But here he was, and she couldn't ignore him now.

"Ready to go?" he asked quietly, his eyes missing nothing as they moved over her slender body.

"Yes. Danny's driving me to the airport," she said.

He only nodded. "Got enough money?" he asked softly.

"For now." She clutched her purse closer. "I... Gil's going to help me get started again, now that I've got my voice back. He has some contacts."

His face froze, but he didn't make any sarcastic comment. "It'll be cold in Houston. Where's your coat?"

"In my closet," she said quietly, meeting his eyes with a bravery she didn't feel. She wanted to throw herself into his arms and cry her heart out. "I don't need it anymore."

She watched his face go even tauter. He knew how much she'd loved the coat, that it was her lucky charm. It had always been precious because he'd given it to her. She was telling him without words that she didn't want him in her life anymore.

"No," he agreed quietly. "Not it, or me. Don't ever look back, baby."

Looking at his rigid features, she remembered the sound of her own voice telling him she loved him, over and over, and she blushed in spite of her efforts. "No," she said. "I won't look back. Good-bye, Cole."

"I never say good-bye," he reminded her. His eyes scanned her face for a long time before he turned away. She watched him until he entered the house and disappeared from view. Then she turned back to the truck where Danny was waiting patiently.

* * *

Houston was alive with nightlife, and Heather told herself she was glad to be in the jeweled city again. She took a cab to her apartment, and decided her first move would be to phone Gil. She hadn't called him from the airport, preferring to surprise him. Now she tossed her shoes off and sat down on the edge of the bed, putting the ranch and Cole and all the unpleasantness to the back of her mind. From now on, she was going to live from day to day. Minutes at a time. And she was going to become, somehow, the biggest, hottest property on the nightclub circuit. She wouldn't let anything stand in her way now. She was going to make it.

"This band is great," Gil told her on the way to the club where the group was rehearsing. "You'll like the guys. They'll like you, too."

She gripped her purse nervously. "I . . . I don't even have my new arrangements," she told him. "There wasn't time to work them up. . . ."

"Don't worry about it. These guys are masters at improvisation. You sing the song to them one time, they'll never have to see sheet music."

"If they're that good, what do they need with me?" She laughed.

"Didn't I tell you?" he asked with a grin. "They may be talented, but they're all *ugly!* They need you to give 'em a little class."

She smiled. "You sure know how to boost a girl's ego."

"That's what I'm here for." He pulled off the street and squeezed his small sports car into a parking spot, cutting the engine. "Okay, angel, we're here. Let's do it."

She opened her door resolutely. "You're on," she said, pretending a confidence she didn't feel.

Gil marched her straight through the club and up to the front where the band was just winding up a number. The musicians were all in their shirtsleeves, some of them smoking. Several were bearded, and the bandleader, in a white T-shirt with "Wild Man!" blazing across it in red letters, needed a haircut badly. They were a far cry from the clean-cut musicians Heather was used to. Wearing a soft cape-sleeved blue velour dress, her hair knotted primly behind her graceful neck, she felt out of place.

"Hi, guys, I brought you a new nightingale," Gil announced.

"Great. Does she sing or do bird calls?" the bandleader asked with a lifted eyebrow. He stared at her over his cigarette, a guitar dangling from a decorative cord around his neck.

"Cute." Gil grinned. "Her name's Heather."

"What else, with that hair?" came the sardonic reply. "I'm Charlie. The drums are Billy Jackson, bass guitar is Jackie Blake, second guitar is Harry White," he said, nodding toward each of his group, "and that's our new guy, Dewey Dan, on the piano. I play lead guitar. They call us the Red Rhythm Band. What do you sing?" he added, narrowing his small brown eyes at her from his far-superior height.

"Whatever you play," she responded gamely.

"A comedienne," came the terse reply. A doubtful pair of brown eyes speared Gil. "Are you sure she knows what she's doing?"

"Go on, give the girl a chance," Gil said impatiently. "How about that soft-rock tidbit I heard you play last week? 'Devil in Ribbons and Lace'... wasn't that it?"

"All right." Charlie shrugged. His eyes glanced off Heather. "Why not?"

He dug for sheet music, found it, and handed Heather a page. "I hope you can sight-read," he muttered.

"I play piano, too," she said with controlled sweetness.

He chuckled, turning back to the band. "Okay, let's see what you can do." He fingered his guitar for tune along with the other band members, gave the downbeat, and they swung into the first throbbing bars of "Devil in Ribbons and Lace." Heather liked the silky beat, the way the prominent rhythm of the drums blended with the rich melody of the guitars and the harmony of the piano. It was a honey of a tune, bursting with promise, and she was already in love with it by the time Charlie gave her the cue. Fires surged in her blood, the remembered sweetness of being on stage, of putting every emotion in her into every song she sang. All her energy was suddenly concentrated into her throat as she belted out the first words of the song in her powerful, clear voice, and the bandleader turned his head abruptly to stare at her as if he'd never seen a singer before. Charlie hadn't even asked for her key, a courtesy any other bandleader would have given her. But the key was just a half step above her own, and the rich contralto filled the room.

"...silky and satin-faced, devil in pretty lace, woman you leave my maaaan alone!" she sang. Her face shone with the pure joy of performing. The energy of the music seemed to enter her bloodstream, and then surge out again in her voice. Her body throbbed in time with the drums. Watching her, any of the men could have been forgiven for thinking she looked like the woman the song was about. There was a wildness under that honey exterior that made her a devil in lace herself.

She forgot the band, Gil, even her surroundings as she put herself inside the song. When it ended on a wild clash of cymbals, she stood there shaking from the emotion she'd released. There was a hush in the club like that of midnight on the range.

As if coming out of a trance, the musicians began to move, putting down their instruments to applaud. Tears formed in Heather's eyes.

"Thanks," she whispered.

"Beauty and talent," Charlie whistled. "What a combination!"

"I told you she was good," Gil put in.

"Anyone who ever looked less like a devil..." Charlie sighed. "I'd love to see her record that song. My God, we'd make the top ten overnight."

"If you're serious about that," Gil told him, sliding a possessive arm around Heather, "I'll go make a couple of phone calls. I told Heather I know the A and R guy over at International; and he owes me a favor. I did a huge feature spread on him a few weeks ago. If he's fool enough to turn us down, I have a few other contacts too."

"I'm serious," Charlie confirmed. "And as far as I'm concerned, the Red Rhythm Band's got a new lead singer—they hire us all or they don't get any of us. Okay, guys?" he asked the group, and they all nodded.

"I hope you're properly impressed," Gil told the stunned singer. "These guys have to turn down gigs. That's how notorious they are. Charlie there was on a national talk show not long ago."

"Oh, you can't do this," Heather protested, flushing. "You might not like the way I do your other songs."

Charlie grinned. "Do you want the job or not?"

"Yes!" Heather cried, her face lighting up, her eyes sparkling.

"Our first show is tomorrow at eight P.M. sharp," he told her. "We'll have to spend the whole day rehearsing."

She pulled up a stool and sat down on it. "So what's the problem?" she asked, linking her hands around her knees.

"And that's how you'll sing," Charlie said suddenly. "We do a couple of slow tunes, for the older folks—over thirty, you know." He chuckled. "You can sing those on the stool."

"Not lying on the piano?" she asked in mock disappointment.

"Why not?" Dewey Dan called out, grinning under his thick glasses. "It'll hold us both!"

"Never fear, my child," Charlie assured her, "I shall protect you from the lecherous advances of that depraved pianist."

"Yeah?" Billy sang out from his drums, his red hair mussed from his exertions. "Who's gonna protect her from you?"

The rest of the band jumped into the argument and Heather stood on the sidelines, laughing. It was good to be singing again after all, and she knew she was going to make it this time. She held on to Gil's sleeve, her eyes wild with the magic of a new beginning. She was going all the way up now! All she had to do was not think about Big Spur.

Heather waited backstage the following night, chewing unconsciously on a long pink fingernail while she waited for the band to end the piece it was playing.

Her heart was pounding while Charlie led up to her introduction, and she could feel her palms sweating. Despite her emotional high the night before, she was afraid of the audience, afraid to stand out there in front of all those sophisticated people and open her mouth. What if she wasn't good enough? What if Charlie had lied? What if she went out there and couldn't make a sound? It was a very real case of stage fright—this was by far the largest audience she had ever sung for—and she had to stifle the urge to run out of the club and forget the whole thing.

" . . . a lovely young talent, Heather!" Charlie concluded. "Let's give her a big hand, ladies and gentlemen!"

The sound of applause gave her just enough confidence to walk gracefully to the front of the band. She thanked the audience, gripped the microphone, focused on the back wall of the club and smiled. She was trembling from head to toe, but when the first throbbing notes sounded on Charlie's lead guitar, confidence began to build inside her. Her blue eyes glittered, her platinum hair swung like molten silver as her slender body in its simple, elegant black dress began to sway sensuously to the beat.

She heard her cue and opened her mouth, and the sound was piercingly clear and sweet. "...woman you leave my maaaaan alone!" She belted out the song, her eyes closing as she let the emotions she felt blaze out of her in a throaty rush. Before she finished, the audience was clapping in time with her. And when she let the dying notes trail away, and bent to the waist over the mike, the applause was deafening. It went on and on and on, and she gaped at the cheering audience with tears running down her cheeks.

"Thanks," she whispered achingly. "Thank you so much."

It was the beginning. Now, she knew she was going to make it.

Chapter Nine

Gil Austin, true to his word, arranged a recording session for Heather and the Red Rhythm Band. Their first single, "Devil in Ribbons and Lace," was released several weeks later and became a runaway local hit. Gil watched it catch on without surprise; his confidence in Heather knew no bounds.

"It's on the top ten in Atlanta." He chuckled, watching Heather over a cup of coffee in one of Houston's exclusive restaurants. The band had just completed a two-week engagement and was scheduled for a one-nighter later that week before they went on the road. This was Heather's first evening off since she'd made her debut, and it felt strange to sit and eat without being nervous about an upcoming performance.

"I still can't believe it...." She laughed as she finished her creamy dessert. "To go so far so fast... And to think, I worked for two years before the accident without ever getting so much publicity."

"This time you've got me to give you a hand," he reminded her.

She smiled at him. She'd gained a little weight, just enough to make her soft curves even softer, and the light was slowly coming back into her blue eyes. She wasn't over Cole, not by a long shot, but she was working her way toward it, thanks to Gil. He pampered her, pushed her, petted her, and never let her forget her ultimate goal. She knew he couldn't be doing it all out of kindness, but she didn't want to question his motives.

"Charlie's helped a lot, too," she told him. "He's even letting me do one of my own songs Friday night. It's called 'Sad, Sad Eyes,' and he did the arranging himself."

Gil studied her quietly, his eyes appraising. "Yours were sad when you came back to me," he told her. "I'm glad the light's back in them again."

She touched his hand lightly. "And you never asked a question. I was grateful for that."

He hadn't had to ask. He knew it had something to do with Everett, who hung over Gil's relationship with Heather like an oversharpened ax, always ready to fall. But he only shrugged and smiled. "I never pry. Unless it's in the line of duty," he added with a grin.

* * *

She should have been on top of the world. She was on her way to being a hot property for the recording studio, she was making money, she was independent of Cole as she'd always wanted to be. But as she'd been on the verge of discovering before her accident, it was like expecting steak and tasting sawdust. It left a bad taste in her mouth.

She couldn't let the band down by giving any less than her best, though. When she walked out on the stage at the Golden Gun for their one-nighter later that week, she put everything she had into her performance. "Devil in Ribbons and Lace" drew a thunderous round of applause. And then they turned down the stage lights, and she climbed onto her stool, oblivious to the couple that quietly walked in and seated themselves at a rear table while the band played the introduction to "Sad, Sad Eyes." It had started out as a blues tune when Heather originally wrote it, but Charlie had given it a bossa nova beat and increased the tempo, so that when Heather sang it now, it raised the blood pressure. Especially when she wore the tight aqua satin dress that made her eyes look like seawater at dawn, her hair a silky platinum cloud.

She was just beginning the song when the sea of people suddenly parted to reveal one silver-eyed, dark face at the rear of the club—a face that was the beginning and end of her world. Cole! She barely noticed Tessa beside him, her eyes riveted to the sensual masculine perfection of him in his dark jacket and striped tie. The sight of him was like a balm to her aching heart after the long, lonely weeks. She almost faltered in mid-note, but training and confidence steeled her nerve. She went on, her sultry voice belting out the song, but there was a new, blinding radiance about her face, a peachy glow that made Gil Austin, in the corner of the room, clench his drink until his fingers turned white.

The music was around her, inside her, and her eyes, full of Cole's dark face, betrayed her to the world as she sang.

"Sad, sad eyes, melancholy eyes, how dark the shadow of your dying love . . . memory and melody can't warm the ashes of . . . the melancholy love that hides . . . behind the sadness of your sad, sad eyes. . . ." She let the sweet melody trail away, the last note of the song dying in the soft silence that followed the band's final bar. All at once, the silence was broken by applause and whistles and cheers, and Heather knew that the song was going to have a popularity of its own. But it didn't matter. Nothing mattered except the sight of Cole sitting there watching her. She had to fight to stop herself from running the length of the room to him with her arms out-stretched.

He doesn't love you, she reminded herself, and all the sweet blazing light visibly died out of her. She finished her last number, a song about love gone wrong, and left the stage. Her knees were trembling when she got to her dressing room. Why was Cole here? Why had he come?

Scant minutes later there was a sharp knock at the door and Heather cringed. "Come in," she called bravely, and found herself meeting Tessa's cold dark eyes in her dressing room mirror.

"Quite the little star, aren't you?" Tessa shrugged, staring indifferently at her surroundings. "I didn't like your act."

Heather shook back her long hair, proceeding to remove her makeup with steady hands. Tessa couldn't hurt her anymore. She'd lost Cole long ago, and there was nothing else she minded losing. Nothing that Tessa could take from her. "I'll cry all the way to the bank," she informed the dark-haired girl with a short laugh. "Strangely enough, Tessa, your opinion doesn't matter to me one way or the other."

That made Tessa's black eyes sparkle wildly. All the envy and jealousy and hatred came boiling to the surface. "I asked Cole to bring me," she told Heather with a false smile. "I wanted you to see him with me. He didn't want to come near the place," she added venomously.

"Don't think I'm any more anxious to see him," came the quiet reply.

"Aren't you?" Tessa propped one long-nailed hand on her hip. "You'll never get Cole," she promised her rival. "I made sure of that."

Heather didn't understand the veiled remark, but she didn't bother with a reply. She finished removing her lipstick and reached for her brush to drag it carelessly through her glorious long hair. "Don't you have somewhere else to go, Tessa?" she asked coolly. "I only entertain my friends backstage."

"Don't play the big star with me!" the other girl screamed at her. "Remember, you're nothing but an outsider at Big Spur now!"

That hit home. It made her burn inside. She turned in her seat and her blue eyes flashed at Tessa, fury making every line of her body taut. "That description fits you better than it will ever fit me," she threw out. "And if you don't get out of my dressing room in the next five seconds, I'll have Johnny's bouncer drag you out of this nightclub through the front door and toss you in the gutter where you belong!"

The other girl's mouth flew open. She'd never heard Heather talk like that. She was absolutely tongue-tied, especially when she read in Heather's eyes that this was no bluff.

Cole chose that moment to walk in the door, making Heather's heart beat wildly in her chest. Tessa, seizing the opportunity, burst into agonized tears. "Oh, Cole, she's cruel!" she moaned, burying her face in his dark jacket. "She called me horrible names and threatened to have me thrown out in the street!"

Cole patted her back absently, glaring over her shoulder at Heather. "Nobody's throwing you anywhere. Go wait for me at the table."

"Of course, darling," she said, sniffing for good measure. She pranced haughtily out the door without a backward glance.

The silence in the room was ominous, like the charged stillness before a hurricane. Heather brushed her hair quietly, avoiding Cole's piercing stare.

"Was it necessary to attack Tessa, who never meant you harm?" he asked coldly.

"Rattlers never mean harm, either, they just strike for the hell of it," she replied. "Surely you could have found another club to take her to? Or couldn't you talk her out of this one?"

He lit a cigarette, watching her in the mirror with narrow, glittering silver eyes. "You look well," he said indifferently. "How's it going?"

She shrugged. "Better than I ever expected. We've got a song climbing the charts and we're about to leave on tour." The sight of him was cutting her to pieces. Her hand clenched the brush handle, and she said untruthfully, "Gil's going, too."

He turned away, his long back stiffening as if she'd struck him. But when he faced her again his expression was as impassive as ever. "Is he? You'll probably need some protection on tour."

Cole, you're killing me! she wanted to scream. But all she could do was swallow down the searing hurt and not let it show.

"Thanks for stopping by to say hello," she said with the same courtesy she'd have shown a stranger. She rose from her seat, a wan smile fixed on her lips.

"It was insanity," he replied, a muscle in his jaw working as his eyes traced her slender body in the revealing dress.

"Then why did you come?" she asked tightly.

A strange smile touched the hard curve of his mouth. "To see if you hated me," he told her.

Her heart hung in mid-air. "No, I don't hate you, Cole."

"I'm sorry about that. It would have been better, for both of us." He crushed out his cigarette and checked his watch. "I'd better get going. Tessa and I need to get some sleep before we fly back in the morning."

Her last hope that she and Cole might have a future together died inside her. Cole and Tessa, together all night; it was more than she could bear.

"No regrets, baby," he said strangely, his face hard. "I've got my ranch and you've got your career."

She nodded. "Music is all I care about," she said, turning her attention to a shiny hairpin on the dresser. Her fingers turned it in the light. "It's the air I breathe."

"I thought Austin was that."

The harshness in his voice brought her face up, and his eyes trapped hers as effectively as a net. That glittering stare burned into her until she could feel her heart pounding in response, the blood rushing to her cheeks.

"God Almighty," he breathed gruffly, "don't look at me like that!"

She tore her eyes away, her lips trembling. She couldn't let herself be drawn to him again, not after the torture of cutting her life away from his. "Go away! I don't want you here!"

There was the sound of boot heels moving behind her, and then strong, hard hands jerked her back against a hard, muscular body. "Like hell you don't," he breathed harshly. "You want the sound and taste and feel of me! God, do you think I'm blind? It was in your eyes when you sang to me tonight. It's shining out of you now like a beacon; it's here in this heartbeat that's shaking your body," he persisted, his hand sliding to rest beneath her soft breast, making her heart race madly under its touch. "You want it so much you're trembling all over!"

The embarrassment was exquisite. Soundless tears slid down her burning cheeks. She tore away from Cole, her eyes burning, and put half the length of the small room between them. "You flatter yourself!" she choked, hating him now, hating herself for her own weakness. Her hands clenched so tightly that the nails bit into her palms.

In her fury, she missed the somber darkness in Cole's silver eyes, the glimpse of pain so sweeping it could not be hidden. She missed the brief hard clenching of his big hands that turned the knuckles white before he rammed them into his pockets. All she saw was the tight smile that lingered on his mouth and the hardness of his face.

"Still want me, Heather?" he asked with calculated cruelty. "Too bad. God knows, I want no part of you. I won't deny that your sweet young body tempted me a bit, but there was never any love in what I felt. I could never love you."

Tears streamed down her cheeks, mirroring a hurt that was bone-deep. She turned stricken eyes to Cole.

"Are you through?" she asked in a choked whisper. "Please, are you through?"

"Pretty near," he agreed casually, his jaw tightening at the sight of her vulnerability. "If I'm getting the point across. Wanting me is a one-way dead-end street. Find someone else to moon over, Heather. I've had about all the love-sick adoration I can stomach for one lifetime."

Her eyes went blank, as if the piercing pain inside her had suddenly turned to numbness. She felt very calm. Cole was telling her he could never love her as a woman, that all she had was a crush on him, and all at once nothing mattered anymore. Nothing mattered. Cole didn't want her.

He scowled at the expression on her face. "Heather?"

She stared at him. "Now, are you through?" she asked expressionlessly.

"Yes," he said tightly. "I'm through. Don't come back to the ranch. Tessa doesn't want you around, and neither do I. If there's anything about the business end of it that you need to know, I'll send you a note. Otherwise, we don't need you. You'd just be underfoot."

He might as well have put a bullet in her, she thought dully. She wouldn't have felt it. "I won't have the time," she told him quietly. "I'm going to be very busy."

He drew a hard breath, turning toward the door, and there was an unfamiliar hesitation in his steps as he paused with his hand on the doorknob, looking back at the pale blond wraith standing so still in the middle of the room. Her paleness, her startling beauty against the darkness of the window behind her was breathtaking. It held him against his will.

"Good-bye," he said tautly.

She didn't answer him. She was afraid her voice would break. She only nodded, mute and aching with an emptiness nothing could fill, not even music. Her eyes were steady on his dark face.

With a muffled curse, he slammed the door behind him. She stared at it for several minutes before she mechanically took off her gown and dressed for the street. She barely noticed when Gil Austin came to take her home, and she didn't say one word to him all the way to her apartment. When he tried to pry some explanation for her behavior out of her, she only smiled and closed the door in his face.

Numb with grief, she walked around in a daze for weeks after that, going through the motions of rehearsal as the band moved on tour from one big city to another. She still gave her all during performances, but as time went by, she began to lose weight. Always delicate, she now became frail. She drove herself at a killing pace. She began to smoke, a habit she'd picked up from Charlie, to his annoyance, and she lived on black coffee and nerves.

"You're killing yourself," Charlie growled, watching her chain smoke one afternoon at rehearsal.

She spared him a cool glance. "What I do with my voice may be your business, but what I do with my life is my own."

"You won't have a life if you keep this up," he persisted. Perching himself on the edge of the piano where she sat, he stared down at her through narrowed brown eyes.

"I'm holding up my end," she said defensively.

"You always have," he agreed, folding his arms across his thin chest. "No argument. But you're beginning to look like a basket case. We're on top right now, you know. I don't kid myself that the boys and I did it alone—it's mostly your looks and talent. But you're getting skeletal, and if you keep smoking those damned things—" he gestured toward the thin white cigarette in her hand "—your voice may not last, either. You've been hoarse a lot these days."

"You taught me how to smoke," she reminded him with a teasing smile.

He returned it. "Shame on me." He mussed her long, silky hair. "Listen. I don't know what's been eating you. I don't pry into anyone's business, 'cause I don't like nosy people either. But if you don't come to grips with whatever's bugging you, you're going to destroy yourself before much longer. All that stress is going to bring you down. And if you won't think of yourself, think about the poor starving musicians you'll put out of work."

That made her smile again. She shrugged. "I guess I have been pretty much in a fog lately," she admitted. She drew in a deep breath and stubbed out the cigarette. "Okay. No more cigarettes. And I'll stop living inside myself."

He grinned. "That's my girl. Think about all that nice money we're going to make. And *Rolling Stone* is sending a reporter out to do a feature spread on you, how about that?"

She mumbled something unintelligible.

"Something you might remember, Heather," he said before he walked away. "Everything passes. Grief, love, happiness, sorrow...everything. Nothing lasts long, and that's a mixed blessing. It might get you through this bad patch to remember it, though."

She bit her lower lip. "Thanks, Charlie," she murmured huskily.

He didn't answer her. She went back to her dressing room, and for the first time since Cole had said good-bye to her, she wept. When the tears stopped, she pulled herself erect and looked at her face in the mirror with a cool, stubborn expression.

"I lived through a killing wreck, and I'll live through this," she told her reflection. "I'll never give Cole the satisfaction of seeing me down for long. From now on, nobody is ever going to make me cry again. Nobody!"

With that idea firmly in mind, she splurged on a new wardrobe and had her long, silky hair cut in a new sexy hairdo that just covered her ears. She grinned as Charlie and the other members of the band moaned and wailed over the change.

"I'm all grown up," she reminded them. "Only little girls walk around with waist-length hair."

"I'll wear black for a month," Dewey Dan mumbled, his bespectacled face lifting accusingly.

"Couldn't they glue it back on?" Billy asked.

"The fans will mob us," Charlie wailed. "They'll think you sold them out. Your hair was your trademark!"

"My new look will be my trademark," she told him with hauteur, indicating the simple elegant lines of her sophisticated gown. The clinging silk fabric was purple with splashes of cool aqua. Draped from one shoulder down across her slenderness like a sari, it emphasized her fairness. It gave her extra maturity. She looked like a woman now, not like a teenager with a crush on any man. The image she projected was that of a young goddess on holiday.

Charlie shook his head. "I love it, don't get me wrong," he told her. "I'm just wondering how the fans are going to react."

"Wait until tonight and we'll all see," she told him with sparkling eyes.

They played to a packed house in one of New York's most exclusive clubs. Heather wore her new gown, and when she perched on her stool in the soft spotlight to do "Sad, Sad Eyes," the daring slit down the front of the dress revealed the graceful curve of one long, tanned leg. There was a hush in the club, almost a feeling of reverence. She put everything she felt into the song, the last of her regret, her heartache, her grief, her loneliness.... It was as if she poured a lifetime of emotion into that one performance, leaving behind nothing but the shell of the girl she'd been. Now she was all elegance and sophistication, poised as she hadn't been before, controlled, cool. And her new look went over like fireworks. As she ended the song the applause burst out, almost deafening, and she had to do an encore before she could get off the stage. It wasn't until later that Charlie told her one of the biggest recording executives in the city had been in that audience. The performance led to a record contract and a week full of personal appearances. She was slated for a talk show later in the year. Overnight, Heather had become the hottest singer in the East. And the band went right to the top with her.

Gil Austin had been following her progress by long distance, but the last night she and the Red Rhythm Band appeared in New York, he showed up backstage to take her out for a late supper.

"I wouldn't have recognized you," he sighed, staring across the table at her as they lingered over coffee. "Miss Sophistication. Where's that long-haired little girl who lived on the edge of her emotions?"

Cole murdered her, she wanted to say, but she only shrugged. "I grew up fast."

He frowned slightly and crossed his arms. "Did you tell your stepbrother I was going on tour with you?" he asked suddenly.

She felt something jerk inside her, but not a movement of her face or body betrayed her inner turmoil. She'd learned to conceal everything now, even her responses. "I don't believe I mentioned it, Gil," she said quietly. "Why?"

He laughed shortly, his eyes dancing. "He called the paper to find out where I was."

That made her angry. What business of Cole's was it who went with her, anyway? "He had no right," she said coldly.

"My editor must have thought he did. He told him. Your stepbrother carries a lot of weight in southeast Texas, didn't you know? He's on a first-name basis with our publisher, and he's got enough money to buy the paper if he wanted to. I had the feeling he wanted my job."

She blinked. "He tried to get you fired?"

"It sounded like it. He doesn't care for me," he said, toying with his fork. His eyes caught hers. "I wonder why he's so antagonistic?"

Nothing showed in her face. "He's been responsible for me for a lot of years, Gil. It's hard to let go."

"Not that hard. And there's no blood relationship between you, is there?" he asked shrewdly.

"He's my stepbrother...."

"That wouldn't stop a man like Everett," he said tightly. "He's rich enough to make his own rules, and I know it. Don't play games with me, Heather. I'd like to know if jealousy has anything to do with his antagonism toward me."

She stared at him. "That comes under the heading of my personal business," she said politely. "I answer to no man. Not to Cole, not to you. I've worked hard to be independent, and I'm not about to give that up now."

"I didn't mean it that way," he argued.

"How did you mean it, then?" she shot back.

He sighed. "Hard as nails, aren't you, baby?"

"Yes, I am, and don't call me 'baby,'" she retorted, her pale blue eyes flashing. "I don't like it."

"Why, because he calls you that?" he returned.

She threw down her napkin and got to her feet. "When you feel like yourself again, do give me a call," she said tightly.

He relented. "Heather, don't walk out on me," he pleaded gently. "I've missed you like hell."

"What a way to show it," she said with a cool smile.

"I'm jealous of him," he admitted under his breath. "God, who wouldn't be? He's got everything: looks, maschismo, money, charm...."

"Not me," she told him. "He may have everything else, but I promise you he doesn't have me. Not now, not ever."

"You hate him, don't you?" he probed.

"I don't feel enough emotion toward him for hatred," she said numbly.

A tiny smile appeared on his lips and the light came back into his eyes. "Let's walk back instead of taking a cab," he suggested, joining her in the aisle. "I feel like howling at the moon tonight."

"I always knew there was a strain of wolf in you," she teased lightly.

They walked outside into the soft night, the freshness of spring discernible despite the traffic and noise.

"The Big Apple." Gil laughed, taking her arm. "I didn't realize how much I'd missed it. I grew up here, you know."

"No, I didn't," she admitted. "Chasing ambulances?"

He shook his head. "Women. I always chased women." He laughed.

They were walking down the street when a teenaged girl and her companion approached Heather hesitantly.

"Aren't you...I mean, are you Heather?" the shorter, darker of the two asked nervously.

She smiled at the girl. "That's me."

The other girl, a bespectacled blond, smiled at her. "Could we please have your autograph? We both want to be singers when we get out of school."

She laughed, flattered and a little embarrassed as she whipped off two signatures. "I hope that's okay," she murmured, handing back the pen they'd given her. "I'm new at this."

"Gee, thanks!" the girls squealed, smiling at her brightly before they hurried away, giggling like conspirators.

"It's like walking with royalty." Gil chuckled.

She grimaced. "I'm not used to it yet, but it sure is flattering. Imagine, somebody wanting my autograph! A few months ago, I couldn't have given it away."

"A few months ago, you weren't the gal you are now," he reminded her with an appreciative glance.

"What a change," he murmured. "Nobody who knew you then would even recognize you now."

She immediately thought of Cole. No, he wouldn't recognize her without the adoration in her eyes or the trembling weakness that had affected her whenever she was near him. She was like ice now. Cole could never touch her again, never hurt her. She smiled coolly as she walked along beside Gil. Despite Emma's worries, she was independent, and she hadn't needed the legacy to accomplish it. If only Emma could have lived to see her stepdaughter now. She caught Gil's hand and held it.

He glanced at her narrowly. "Is that an invitation?" he asked.

She smiled at him. "What do you think?" she asked in her huskiest tone.

He pulled her close and tucked her under his arm. "I think it's my lucky night. I've waited a long time for a green light from you."

"What you're getting is a yellow one," she said quietly.

"Proceed with caution?" he teased. "Suits me, honey, I like to take my time anyway. I won't rush you."

The words triggered a memory she didn't want, the slowness of Cole's lovemaking, the devastating leisure of his hard, warm kisses against her mouth, the aching mastery of his hands on her soft body....

"Let's go dancing!" she said suddenly.

"But it's past midnight!" he protested.

"There's a disco across the street. Come on," she pleaded, pouting. "Live a little."

"God help my poor old bones, I'll give it a try. Come on, you minx, lead me into it!" He laughed, following as she tugged him along with her.

Spring was turning the grass green in the pastures, and roundup on Big Spur had just begun when Mrs. Jones drove the station wagon out to the holding pens to find Cole.

"It must be something important to get you behind the wheel of a car," he remarked with a faint smile as he studied the matronly, gray-haired woman.

"Yes, sir, it is," Dessie Jones agreed, grimacing at the steering wheel. "That Andrews man is up at the house waiting to see you, and I couldn't raise anybody on the radio to come tell you."

"Andrews," he murmured. "My mother's lawyer?"

"The same."

"Move over, Dessie, I'll drive you back."

"Oh, would you?" she asked, heaving her ample bulk to the passenger side. "I do hate these mechanical contraptions."

"I'll remember that, the next time you ask me for a new food processor for the kitchen," he said, putting the station wagon in gear.

"Oh, now, Mr. Cole!" she protested.

They were back at the house in no time and Cole took the steps two at a time, wondering impatiently what Andrews wanted. The will had gone through probate long ago, surely he hadn't found a new one!

Bob Andrews looked as disheveled and haphazard as ever. He stood when Cole came into the living room and extended his hand. "Good to see you, Cole," he said pleasantly. "Sorry to come at such a bad time."

Cole tossed his hat on the bar and reached for glasses. "I needed a break," he replied. "Care for a drink?"

"Scotch on the rocks for me, and thanks. It was a long, dry ride."

The older man joined him on a bar stool, and they sat sipping their drinks for a minute before Andrews opened his briefcase, fumbled for a moment and produced an envelope.

He tossed it down on the smooth, glassy surface of the bar. "I've been sorely remiss about this," he said, "and I won't blame you if you want to throw a punch at me. Emma made me promise to give it to you as soon as possible after her death, but to tell the truth, it got misplaced in my office and only surfaced a week ago. I don't suppose it was anything too urgent, but in case it might be, I came as soon as I could."

Cole studied the white envelope. His name was scrawled on it in Emma's spidery hand, and it was sealed. "When did she give you this?" he asked quietly.

"The day before you left for Nassau," he replied. "Came to my office in the afternoon, very somber, not like Emma at all. She said she'd been to the doctor that morning, and she wanted to make sure her will was in order. I asked if anything was wrong, and she just laughed and made light of it. But apparently she had some kind of premonition.''

''Apparently.'' Cole took another swallow of his drink and tore open the envelope. Inside there was one typed sheet of paper. He remembered with a wistful smile how Emma had typed letters using only one finger. She didn't trust her handwriting, but it would take her forever to peck out a sentence on the typewriter. As he unfolded the paper and began to read, his silver eyes narrowed.

''Dear Cole,'' Emma had written, ''I've just been to see my doctor, and he says my indigestion is actually congestive heart failure.'' Cole's eyebrows shot up. ''I have very little time left, he says. I'm not afraid to die, my dear, but I want to know that my affairs are in order in case it happens sooner than I expect.

''First,'' she continued, ''I want to explain why I left half the estate to Heather. Big Spur was Jed Shaw's long before it was yours and mine, and Heather should have had it all probably. But you put a lot of work into building it up, and I didn't think she'd mind letting part of it go to you. She's not going to like being dependent on you for money, and that's another reason I divided the ranch between you. But my best reason was that I'm doing my best to play Cupid. I can't think of anything that would please me more than having you and Heather discover that you love one another. I had that kind of love with your father, Cole. There was never anyone who could match Big Jace, not even Jed Shaw. I cared for Jed in

my own way, but all I could give him were the crumbs
left over from my first marriage, and I'm afraid he
knew it.

"Big Jace was the only man for me, just as I was the
only woman for him. Don't ever let anyone tell you
there was something going on between him and Deidre
Shaw. A great many people knew that she made a play
for your father. But I give you my solemn word that
nothing happened, ever. I'd have known if it did. Jace
loved me until he died, and there was never another
woman. Nor was there any kind of relationship between myself and Jed Shaw before we married. I
rushed into marriage with him more for Heather's
sake than my own. I could have lived with the memory of Big Jace for the rest of my life and it would have
been more than enough."

Cole's hand jerked on the page, and his eyes flashed
wildly.

"Of course, I don't want to push either of you into
anything. Heather may not be in love with you, or vice
versa. In that case, I've done the right thing to make
her financially independent of you. Of course, if
things work out, there won't be a problem, you'll have
the ranch together. Be kind to her, Cole, whatever
happens. She worships you. Don't grieve for me. I'll
be with Jason again, and wherever he is, that will be
Heaven. I love you. Mother."

Cole's eyes closed on a wave of panic so intense he
felt his knees were going to buckle. If this letter told
the truth, and of course it did, he'd driven Heather
away for nothing. For nothing, damn Tessa!

"Are you all right?" Andrews asked warily.

Cole opened his eyes again, his face rigid and pale, his body frozen. He picked up his drink and drained the glass in one quick swallow.

"I have a horrible feeling that I've caused some disaster," Andrews murmured regretfully.

"Call it fate," Cole ground out, crushing the letter in one lean, powerful hand.

After seeing the attorney to the door, he marched into the kitchen, his eyes throwing off sparks, his face set in an expression Mrs. Jones hadn't seen in years. "I need to ask you something," he said without preamble, watching her deft hands pause in the middle of chopping onions for the quiche she was making.

"Yes, sir," she replied.

"You told me once that you suspected something was going on between my father and Deidre Shaw...."

"Heavens no!" She gasped, horrified.

He blinked. "You said my father couldn't help it...."

"He couldn't help that Mrs. Shaw hunted him," she replied quickly. "I thought you knew about that night when he threatened to tell her husband what she was doing, Mr. Cole. It was one time when Mr. Shaw was away. She made up some reason to get Mr. Everett over here to Big Spur. She was throwing herself at his feet when I came in. Your father, God bless him, was almost purple with rage. He informed her in no uncertain terms that he loved his wife and wanted nothing to do with her." She watched all the hardness go out of him, to be replaced with a black sadness that was more painful to behold. "It wasn't my place to tell anyone, you understand," she added helplessly.

"No, of course it wasn't." He shrugged. "I appreciate your telling me the truth."

"Is something wrong? Is that what made Mr. Andrews come out here, if you don't mind my asking?"

"Yes, something is very wrong," he agreed, turning. "And I only hope I can put it right."

Two days later, he sat in the audience at the club in New Orleans where Heather and the Red Rhythm Band were appearing and watched her belt out a soft-rock song with a professionalism she'd never have managed before the accident. He didn't like that short haircut she was sporting, but her new sophisticated image drew his eyes. She was so obviously a woman now, not the child he'd driven away from him.

He studied her slender body. She was wearing a silver gown that plunged and clung to every soft curve and Cole knew she was working a subtle witchcraft on every man in the audience. Her voice was better than ever, haunting, lovely, and he could easily understand her growing fame. This club, the most exclusive in New Orleans, would be her last stop before she went back to Houston.

He had come to talk her into the proposition he had in mind. He shifted restlessly in his elegant dark evening clothes, feeling uncomfortable. He hadn't dressed like this for ages, not since he'd last seen Heather, and he would gladly have traded the confining suit for his jeans and denim shirt. He'd driven himself hard lately, putting in unnecessary hours helping the men with round-up, but he'd needed the physical activity badly. Sitting at his downtown office hadn't been enough to keep his mind busy.

His heart turned over at the thinness of Heather's body. She'd lost weight, a lot of it, and her face was drawn beneath her makeup. His jaw clenched when he remembered what he'd said to her the last time. He wondered if she'd ever be able to forgive him, even as he realized that he could never tell her what he had thought or why he had acted as he had. His pride wouldn't let him.

Heather, oblivious to everything but the song she was singing, uttered the last poignant words and then bowed in the spotlight as Charlie led the band into her theme song, "Devil in Ribbons and Lace." She turned, blowing a kiss to the band and then to the wildly applauding audience, before she walked off-stage.

She felt lonely when she closed the dressing-room door behind her. Gil was back in Houston now, and she missed him terribly. Nothing had really changed in their relationship, but he was a good friend and she enjoyed his bubbling company. Now that he wasn't around, she'd have nothing to do. New Orleans was a lovely city at night, but not for a woman alone. She'd go back to her hotel room and stare at the walls, drink too much black coffee and sleep too little, as usual.

A soft knock at the door brought her out of her depression. "Come in, it's open!" she called with forced cheer.

The door swung open and her heart turned a double flip in her chest when she saw Cole standing behind her in the mirror—dressed in dark evening clothes that emphasized his rugged masculinity. His face was harder than she remembered it, his eyes glittering. But the expression on his dark face didn't give away what he was feeling. She had thought she was over him until then; she'd thought she could be in the same room with him and feel nothing. But her breath was already coming in uneven gasps, and she knew her hands would tremble if they weren't clasped tightly in her lap.

"Hello, Cole," she managed quietly.

He ran his eyes over her with a slow, thorough boldness that made her pulse pound. "Hello."

She lifted her face proudly. "Is something wrong at the ranch?" she asked with deceptive coldness. "I don't flatter myself that you'd come all this way just to see me."

"Why not?" he asked.

She laughed mirthlessly and turned back to her mirror to dab cold cream on her face. "I don't need to tell you. You made it very clear that you don't want me around, remember?"

His eyes closed briefly, but she missed his moment of anguish because she couldn't bring herself to look at him. "Where's Austin?" he asked pointedly. "Is he with you?"

"You don't have the right to ask me that," she told him levelly, flashing a glance at him.

"Probably not." He lit a cigarette with quick, jerky motions. "He didn't go on tour with you. You lied about that."

"Of course." She laughed. "I tell lies, I throw myself at men—"

"Oh, God, don't!" he bit off, whirling on his heel to stare out the darkened window, his back rigid with pain.

She shrugged, puzzled by his strange behavior, but she was getting herself under control now, and she wanted no part of him. Cole meant heartache and she didn't want any more of that.

"You still haven't told me why you came," she remarked.

He took a long draw from the cigarette. "You've got a vacation coming up after this performance, don't you?" he asked. His eyes had darkened slightly, but his face was as impassive as ever.

She eyed him warily. "Yes. Why?"

"Why don't you spend it at the ranch?" he asked carelessly.

She flinched as if he'd struck her, and a wave of undefinable emotion rippled over his pained features when he saw her involuntary reaction. She dropped her eyes. "I'm not welcome there," she reminded him.

"Heather, for God's sake . . . !" he burst out.

Her pale eyes jerked up, serenely cool. "You're not getting another free shot at me, Cole, or Tessa either. I've had all I'm going to take from either of you. Maybe you've conveniently forgotten what you said to me the last time you came to one of my performances, but I'll live and die trying to. You cut me into ribbons that night. I'm not about to give you a second chance."

He froze at the words, scowling, his eyes narrowed.

"Tessa's in Paris," he said through tight lips, his expression unreadable.

"How terrible for you," she returned. "What do you want me for, a substitute? I never did like being second best, despite what you think of me."

"You don't know what I think," he said quietly.

"Don't I?" Her soft voice was bitter. She grabbed some tissues and mopped the cold cream and makeup from her face in one smooth motion. "You've made it plain enough, haven't you?"

"Circumstances can cause people to do a hell of a lot of strange things, Heather," he reminded her.

She didn't even answer him. The memories were hurting too much.

"I'm not asking you into my bed," he growled. "I'm offering you a quiet place to rest, that's all. Period."

She sighed deeply. That's all he had to offer, and she knew it. "I don't think it would be a good idea."

"Damn it!" he burst out, jerking around. He took an exasperated draw from the cigarette and his lips made a thin line. "Were you always this stubborn, or have you been taking lessons?"

"Look who's talking," she replied lightly. The words slipped out unconsciously, and so did a faint smile. He caught his breath at the light in her lovely face as he stared at her across the room.

She looked away from that intense stare, puzzled by his expression. "Will sweet Tessa be there?" she asked.

He stared at her straight back. "No."

"Can I bring Gil?"

"What for?" he growled. "I don't need a comedy act."

She turned. "Why do you want me to come?"

He whirled on his heel and crushed out the cigarette. "God knows," he muttered under his breath. "Forget it."

"Cole?"

"What!" he ground out.

She studied him quietly, trying to understand this new attitude. He wanted her home and it was galling to him that he had to ask her—that much showed. He'd rather make it an order, but the days were gone when he could command her to do anything and he knew it. The knowledge was evident in his furrowed brow and clenched jaw. He didn't like her independence, and she was suddenly grateful that he didn't hold the purse strings. Cole could be a tyrant in this mood.

"Cole, I can't take any more abuse from you," she said very calmly. Her eyes showed the old hurt for an instant before she could disguise it and he read it there. "I'm living on my nerves as it is. I don't think I've ever really gotten over your last visit. You said it yourself, you've got your ranch and I have my career. I think we'll both be better off if we go our separate ways."

"Do you really?" he asked in a goaded undertone. His eyes flashed and he took a deliberate step toward her.

She backed away from him, all her composure dropping away, her eyes wild, her lips trembling. "No!"

He froze where he stood, drawing in a deep, harsh breath. "Oh, my God, don't look like that," he whispered.

"Don't touch me," she breathed unsteadily. "Don't ever."

"I'm not coming any closer, baby," he said gently, speaking as he would to a frightened filly. "It's all right, I won't hurt you."

She caught her lower lip in her teeth and stared at him, breathing quickly. If he came any closer, she would call for help. She didn't know what would happen now if he took her in his arms, and she didn't want to find out. He was a closed chapter in her life. She wanted to leave it like that. Her heart wouldn't survive another dose of Cole.

He looked as if she'd struck him across the face, but he didn't retaliate. "Maybe it's too soon," he murmured, his eyes studying her stiff face. "I'm impatient," he added with a hint of a smile. "It's never been easy for me to wait for things."

She relaxed a little. Her body seemed to slump against the wall while her mind tried to make some sense of his remark.

"Come home with me," he said gently. "Bring the damned journalist if you want to," he added gruffly.

She drew in a slow breath. The ranch would give her the opportunity to rest a little, away from telephones and fans and booking agents.... She glanced up at Cole, but his face was unreadable. If she took Gil along, she'd be safe from Cole. And that was what she wanted, wasn't it?

"All right," she said gently, glancing up at him and then away. "We'll come," she agreed, hoping Gil wouldn't mind being volunteered.

Cole's mouth turned up in a strangely enigmatic smile. "I'll take you riding."

"Gil and I will like that," she said deliberately.

"We'll see." He turned on his heel, pausing at the door. "Next week? What day?"

"Friday?"

He nodded. "Catch a charter to Victoria. I'll drive in and pick you up—or fly over, if the boys don't need the plane for roundup."

"Isn't that over by now?" she asked curiously.

"There are two areas I haven't checked in some time. It's a big ranch, baby," he reminded her.

"I remember."

His eyes swept over her one last time. "Friday." And he was gone, like Mephistopheles, smug at having gotten his own way. And Heather was more uncertain now than ever. How was she going to cope with both Cole and Gil at the same time? It would be like spending a vacation in the midst of two warring tribes.

She got up and began to dress. She'd have to call Gil and tell him what she'd gotten them into.

Chapter Ten

To say Gil was upset was an understatement.

"Did you have to obligate us?" he grumbled, eyeing her accusingly. "I wanted to take you down to my folks' place in West Palm Beach that week."

She was shocked. She hadn't realized things were moving that fast, and although she submitted docilely when Gil kissed her, she'd never been able to return his passion. She hadn't imagined he was getting so serious, and her spirit balked at involvement. She didn't want ties. That was one thing she'd learned from Cole, not to let people get too close. She wouldn't be hurt that way.

"Gil, you might have asked me about it," she returned gently.

He grimaced. "I meant to, but I wasn't sure how you'd react." His green eyes narrowed on her face. "Heather, I want to marry you."

Her soft lips parted. She didn't know how to cope with that without hurting his feelings. But her reluctance showed, and he frowned.

"No go, huh?" he asked heavily. He sighed, and forced a smile. "Okay, I'll give you a while longer. Never let it be said that I slipped through your fingers. Just look at what a bargain you'd be getting. I'm handsome, witty, intelligent, and I have all my own teeth!"

She laughed in spite of herself. "I like you so much," she told him. "But don't rush me, okay? I'm not ready to meet your folks and start looking for a house in the country. I've only just learned what it is to be independent. Let me enjoy it for a few years."

He shrugged. "I won't give up," he warned.

"Okay," she smiled. "Come to Big Spur with me?"

"It looks like I'll have to," he told her. "If Everett's after you."

She flushed. "He's not after me."

"No? Why did he fly all the way to New Orleans to see you when he knew you'd be back in Houston today?" he asked sharply.

"I don't know."

"Don't you?"

"Gil, stop it!" she burst out, her eyes blazing. "Cole's part of my life, just like Big Spur, and I do own half the ranch. I can't turn my back on either one of them. Don't ask me to."

"I've seen the way he looks at you," he remarked tightly, and for an instant his kind green eyes weren't kind at all. "Just as if you were one of his possessions. A bright jewel to hold in his hand."

"Cole's that way about everything in his life," she said. "It's the way he's made."

"But you don't belong to him anymore," Gil protested.

She turned away from his probing eyes. "I'm hungry. How about going dutch with me at the fish place on the corner?"

He hesitated, letting all the antagonism drain out of him in a rough sigh. He ruffled his blond hair irritably. "Okay. Fish it is."

She was packed and ready to go early Friday morning, feeling a sense of anticipation as well as some misgivings about the trip. She didn't want to go. But part of her went weak thinking about the time she'd have with Cole. Being around him for a few days, watching him, listening to his deep, measured voice late at night . . . the hunger for him had started again, like a soft, building melody in her blood, singing despite her efforts to mute it.

She was waiting for Gil to pick her up when the phone rang, and her face fell as she listened.

"We've got to be in Miami by six o'clock tonight," Charlie was telling her. "I'm sorry, honey, I know you were looking forward to that time off, but this gig was too much to turn down," and he rattled off a figure that made her whistle. "See what I mean?"

"I see," she murmured, disappointment in her soft voice. "I'm already packed, I'll just meet you at the airport. Okay?"

"Okay, doll. Sorry," he said again. "But it'll only be for a week, I promise."

She called Gil at his apartment to tell him the news.

"How terrible for Everett." He laughed bitterly. "You'll never guess what a coincidence this is. I've been ordered to New York on a story that someone else was slated to cover. How's that for convenience? You would have been headed for Branntville on your own."

She flushed. "Cole wouldn't have done that," she assured him. "He wouldn't be so underhanded."

"Care to bet? Ask him," he challenged.

She called Cole, her senses quickening as she heard his deep voice on the other end of the line.

"I can't come," she said, not prolonging it. "Charlie accepted a week's engagement at the Coconut in Miami. We're on our way now."

There was a harsh, muffled curse. "Why now?" he ground out. "Damn it, you've pushed yourself until you're nothing but skin and bones already."

She knew that was true; she was feeling the effects of the pressure, but she hadn't any choice. "Cole, did you have Gil sent to New York?" she asked.

There was a brief hesitation. "Yes," he said. He'd never lied to her. She knew he never would, whatever tensions there were between them.

"That was underhanded," she said coolly.

"Men do underhanded things when they're desperate, baby," he replied heavily. "I wanted you here damned bad."

"That's sad, then, because I'll never agree to come again," she told him flatly. "I said with Gil and I meant with Gil. I won't stay at Big Spur alone with you!"

"Afraid of me, baby?" he murmured sensually.

"Not on your life!" she replied.

But he only laughed. "I'll be in touch."

"Don't bother. I won't come!"

"We'll see about that."

She slammed the receiver down without saying good-bye.

Miami was blazing hot, but the evenings were chilly, especially along the stretch of private beach where Heather liked to take her late-night walks. She glanced over her shoulder toward Collins Avenue and the row of deluxe hotels that lined the beach. She came out here after every performance to get away from the bright lights and noise and the smell of alcohol. She wanted Big Spur. She wanted Cole. She wanted to run into his arms and have him hold her, need her, want her again as he had in Nassau. She wanted to be safe and secure in his embrace, and never leave it. To sit beside him on the big front lawn in the summer and watch their children play. Life without Cole was colorless, and Gil made no difference. She was alone without Cole. Alone and aching and wounded.

She didn't bother to wear a wrap, and she was barefoot. By the time she got back to her room, she was sneezing. The next morning she could barely get out of bed, and her throat felt like raw meat. She didn't dare tell Charlie what she'd done, because he'd never let her on the stage. And this was the last night of their engagement. She'd prop herself up and make it somehow.

She gargled with mouthwash, took two aspirin, ate nothing and went onstage. She wore her simple black dress and a tacked-on smile, with a flush on her face that was nothing but fever. She walked into the spotlight when she was introduced, perched herself on the stool, began to sing . . . and collapsed.

When she came to, after a long night of strange dreams with people running and voices calling, she opened her eyes in her own room at Big Spur.

It was a shock to find herself there, and she wondered for an instant if she was dreaming . . . until she turned her head and found a pair of bloodshot silver eyes staring straight into hers.

"Back from the dead?" Cole asked with a faint smile.

"Where's Gil?" she asked tightly. "And what am I doing here?"

His eyes flashed at the first question, but his voice was controlled, calm. "I don't give a damn where he is," he said, leaning back in the chair, his pale blue cotton shirt open at the throat, his dark hair mussed. "Your bandleader called me from Miami and told me what happened. I flew down and brought you home."

She studied him quietly. He looked as if he hadn't moved or slept all night long, but he was just as handsome as ever, all man.

"Have I been out long?" she asked drowsily.

"Two days, more or less. Want something cold to drink?"

"Anything," she said with a weak smile.

"Iced tea, then." He lifted a glass out of an ice bucket. It was full of chipped ice and dark amber tea. He handed it to her.

She sat up in bed to take it and blushed furiously when she realized that, apart from her very brief panties, she had nothing on. She caught the coverlet just in time to save her modesty.

Her fingers went white on the coverlet. "Didn't I have a gown?" she asked shakily, her senses swimming at the thought of Cole's eyes on her body.

"You were sweating with fever," he murmured. "The doctor in Miami gave you some antibiotic capsules and a shot, but the medicine was taking its own sweet time to work, and you had a temperature of a hundred and three. I had to sponge you every fifteen minutes. It was a waste of time to take your nightgown off every time."

She lowered her embarrassed eyes to the bed. "Was I that feverish?"

He nodded. "You had me worried, Sunflower," he said, using the old nickname he'd given her in happier times.

She sipped the tea, eyeing him over the rim of the glass. His eyes were quiet and kind. "Thank you for taking care of me," she said after she swallowed the cold, sweet liquid.

"It was..."

"If you say 'my pleasure,' I'll hit you," she interrupted.

A corner of his chiseled mouth curled up. "That's exactly what I was going to say. And please do try to hit me. I'd enjoy watching you climb out of that bed."

"I'll just bet you would," she shot back, flushing.

"You didn't have any business in Miami in the first place," he said, leaning back in his chair to study her solemnly. "You're run-down. Too much pressure, too much of the time. You never rest."

"When have you ever rested?" she asked pointedly. "If we're going to split hairs, you don't look like the epitome of good health, either."

He smiled again. "I've had a lot on my mind."

"You always do. You never let yourself really relax," she reminded him.

He frowned, memory clouding his silver eyes. "I could never afford to at first," he said quietly. "And then it got to be a habit."

"Tell me about those early years, before you came to live at Big Spur," she murmured, glancing at him over her tea glass.

He laughed softly. "I don't much like remembering them. You were born to antique furniture and silver services. My father worked damned hard, but the best he could manage was a small feedlot and one prize Brahma bull that made other breeders green with envy. Ironic that one of the horses got him, and not that damned mean bull."

"Emma said that Big Jace used to breed broncs for the rodeo circuit."

He nodded. "It was one of those he was riding when he was killed. I'll never forget that day. I'd just driven Mother into town, and we went flying past the corral, wondering what all the commotion was about. Mother fainted."

"I remember that big Brahma bull. Dad used to talk about him all the time, before he and Emma married," she recalled with a drowsy smile.

He nodded. "She accused him of marrying her for the bull. He was a champion."

Her eyes caressed his hard face, seeing the years of struggle reflected in it at that moment. "You've never talked to me like this before," she said suddenly.

"You were a child, Heather," he reminded her with a patient smile.

"You're still trying to treat me like one," she mused.

The smile left his face. "No," he said. "I'm definitely not trying to treat you like a child."

She stared at him, her heart pumping wildly, her eyes wide and anxious.

"You were a beautiful child," he said softly, his eyes studying her, as if he could see through the bedclothes. "You're even more beautiful now. All of you. As pink and soft as a rose petal, as perfect as any goddess," he murmured, his gaze stopping at the spot where her hands held the coverlet to conceal her bareness.

"I can't bear the thought of you...touching me like that while I was unconscious!" she burst out, the words rushing from her involuntarily. She was dizzy at the thought of his lean, beautiful fingers on her soft skin.

Something flashed in his eyes and he rose slowly out of the chair, his expression hard. It was clear he'd misunderstood her words. "I've given you more than enough cause to hate me," he said heavily. "But I didn't realize my touch was suddenly repulsive to you." He turned and started out the door. "Mrs. Jones is downstairs if you need anything. Just bang on the table," he said, jerking the door shut behind him without looking back at her.

"Cole!" she cried after him.

But his footsteps were already dying away down the hall.

She lay back against the pillows with a sigh. Maybe it was better this way after all. If Cole knew how vulnerable she was to him, it wouldn't do at all.

He didn't visit again all that day, and when Mrs. Jones came back to pick up the supper dishes, her wide face was perturbed.

"Hasn't eaten a bite all day," she muttered to Heather. "Snaps at everybody who goes near him.... Miss Heather, he acts like an old wolf with an arrow sticking through one leg. I know he was worried about you at first, and he sat with you the whole time you were sick. But you're better now. Why isn't he?"

Heather's eyes closed briefly. She must have hurt him. Cole never showed anything, but she knew his moods very well.

She threw back the bedcovers and got to her feet. The old cotton gown she'd found in a drawer reached halfway between her knees and her ankles, shapeless but covering. She wobbled to the closet, dragged out an old silk dressing gown, and wrapped her thin body in it. "I'll go see about him," she told Mrs. Jones.

"You shouldn't be up."

Heather only smiled. "I'll never get better lying on my back. I've got engagements to meet, and the sooner I start moving around, the faster I'll heal."

"Don't you fall down these steps," the housekeeper warned, going down them first so that if Heather slipped she'd be able to catch her.

"I won't."

She held on to the polished mahogany banister all the way down, and Mrs. Jones breathed an audible sigh of relief when they were on the ground floor. She patted the younger woman on the shoulder and ambled away toward the kitchen.

Heather paused at the entrance to Cole's den, tapping lightly on the heavy oak door.

"Come in," he growled.

She opened the door and went into the dark, masculine room, closing the door gently behind her to stare at the heavily lined face of the man bending over the desk. "Cole?" she asked softly.

He lifted his eyes, surprise in them. "What are you doing down here?"

She stared at him, frowning slightly as she tried to find the words. "I . . . I didn't mean it the way it came out," she stammered.

He blinked at her. "Would you like to try again?" he asked, laying down his pen.

"What...what I said upstairs," she murmured. She pressed back against the door, watching him rise and come toward her.

He stopped in front of her, his hands in his pockets, his shirt carelessly unbuttoned over that thatch of dark curling hair on his bronzed chest. He smelled of cologne and soap, and her eyes helplessly lifted to his clean-shaven face.

"You don't want me to touch you," he said quietly. "I know that, and I'm not going to. You don't have to have excuses. It doesn't matter."

"It wasn't...an excuse, exactly," she faltered. She sighed wearily. "I'm so tired."

"You shouldn't be down here. It's too soon."

She smiled faintly. "I know. But I couldn't let you go on thinking that your touch repulses me. It's not true, and we've never lied to each other. Not ever."

He nodded. "What *did* you mean?" he asked with narrowed eyes as he studied her pale, drawn face.

She stared straight ahead at his hard chest. Her heartbeat was frantic. "It...made me feel strange to think about being...being touched so intimately... by you," she managed in a thin, unsteady voice.

"I didn't touch you the way I did in Nassau," he murmured. "But I want to, Heather. I want to kiss every soft inch of you, and I want you wide-awake and looking at me when it happens."

His words conjured up pictures that made her knees tremble. She stared up at him, fear and excited anticipation mingling in her soft blue eyes.

"Oh, Heather," he murmured softly. "I've hurt you in ways I never meant to. It's going to take time for the wounds to heal, I know that. But don't push me away, baby. Don't shut me out of your life completely. If we can't make it any other way, then let's go back seven years and pick up the threads. I don't want to lose you again."

He sounded lonely for an instant, but she decided that it must have been a trick of her mind, because his face was as impassive as ever.

"Then stop trying to make a puppet out of me, Cole," she pleaded softly. "I'm not a child; I have a life of my own, a career that I want very much. Allow me the privilege of being myself. Stop trying to make me over to your specifications."

He smiled down at her. "Is that what I've been doing?" he asked.

"Most of my life," she agreed with a hint of tartness. "Incorrigible man."

He chuckled. "You're pretty incorrigible yourself, Sunflower," he remarked. "So now we're equals, is that what all this is leading up to?"

"That's right," she agreed.

He drew a long, deep breath. "You're asking a lot from me."

Her eyes danced. "You wouldn't want to be accused of male chauvinism, now, would you?" she teased.

"Absolutely not," he returned, laughing. "Come on, I'll walk you back upstairs."

She followed him out the door and up the steps, and he went slowly, turning back periodically to make sure she was all right. He left her at the door to her room, his face thoughtful.

"I've got a new foal in the barn. If you're up to it tomorrow, I'll take you down to see him," he told her.

Her eyes lit up. "I'd love it."

"Not early," he said. "I've got a meeting at the office with a meat packer."

"I'll sleep late." She laughed.

"You need a lot of late mornings and early nights to get rid of those circles under your eyes," he said gently. "And I don't like seeing so little flesh on your bones, either."

"I'll eat more," she promised, turning away.

"Sleep well, baby."

It took an effort to walk into the barn and stroll casually down the aisle to look at Cole's new foal in its spotless stall. Old memories haunted her.

Cole hooked his boot over the railing and leaned his forearms on the stall gate to study the wobbly little creature nursing inside.

"I've named him Jackrabbit," he told her. "He has such long ears and legs, it seems to suit."

"Yes, it does," she admitted with a smile.

Her gaze went back to the doorway of the barn, and his eyes followed it. "It seems like a long time ago, doesn't it?" he asked quietly. "I was too rough, but what I was feeling made me that way. I'd been fighting it for a long time."

She tore her eyes away and let them drop to the wood shavings on the ground. "I think I'd been fighting my feelings for just as long."

He chuckled softly at the admission. "I went around in a black mood for days after that. You were so young, and I was eaten up with guilt. I hated what I'd done. But the minute I touched you again, all my good intentions went right out the window, and in Nassau..."

Heather turned and started toward the door, her heart going mad. She didn't want to think about Nassau. It had been too devastating, and even now she couldn't trust Cole because of it. Not knowing why he'd changed so abruptly, she couldn't be certain he wouldn't seduce her and then be cruel all over again. She couldn't risk it.

"Heather?"

She stopped, with her back to him. "Yes?"

"There was a reason for the way I treated you," he said quietly. "Someday I may even be able to tell you what it was, but right now it wouldn't serve any purpose at all."

"You were cruel, Cole."

There was a long pause. "Yes," he agreed in a hunted tone. "I thought I had to be."

"And I thought there was something special between us," she whispered in a choked tone, "but you made it all too clear that I was mistaken!"

"Oh, God," he said heavily. "Heather, don't look back. Things are too strained right now to dredge up all the ghosts. Let's just leave the past where it is for now."

She turned around and stared down the aisle at him. "I can't—I remember too clearly how much you hurt me then, Cole, and I don't think I'll ever forget it." She turned away and walked out of the barn, pausing at the white paddock fence to watch the quarter horses prancing over the green grass.

Several minutes passed before he came up beside her and spoke again, bringing up a neutral topic of conversation. "I'd like to run breeding stock here," he said, gesturing toward the long stretch of land that rolled off toward the horizon.

"We could breed racehorses?" she asked.

He smiled at her. "Would you like that?"

She shrugged. "I like horses."

"If we ran that kind of operation, you'd have to come home. You couldn't zip all over the world on tour. I'd have to have someone to help me entertain buyers." He reached out and tugged a short lock of her hair. "You wouldn't like that, would you?"

She bit her lip and fought for control. The light touch of his fingers had her trembling already. "I... I've worked very hard to get where I am."

"I know," he growled. "God forbid that you should have to live without applause and leering male eyes!"

"Cole!" she gasped at the anger in his voice.

He drew in a harsh breath. "I know, I'm not being fair. I don't feel particularly fair." His fingers lingered at her scalp, testing the soft texture of her silky hair. "I don't like it short like this," he murmured. "In Nassau, I remember tangling my hands in it while I made love to you...."

She drew in a sharp breath, finding her eyes held in bondage by his, her heart pounding wildly with emotion.

"Do you remember how it felt?" he murmured, moving closer so that she could feel the blazing warmth of his body. "Skin against skin, with the breeze from the Caribbean blowing and the sound of the waves.... You moaned, but not in pain, remember?"

Her eyes closed. "Oh, yes, I remember," she whispered achingly, "and I don't want to! Cole, this isn't fair."

"What I feel isn't fair," he growled, crushing her hand against his broad chest. "You're trying to make me back into some kind of safe older brother, but it won't work; I don't want that kind of relationship with you. Let's get that straight right now."

Her heart went wild. "What...what do you want?"

His fingers tilted her chin up and he bent, taking her mouth very gently under his hard lips, tasting it softly, sweetly, in a kiss that had nothing of passion in it. She could feel the warmth of his mouth against hers, but he didn't try to force her lips apart or deepen the kiss in any way. He drew back seconds later as if he was afraid of bruising her with even the lightest pressure. "That's what I want," he said quietly.

She gazed up at him, her eyes full of reawakening dreams and silent fears. "Don't hurt me again, Cole," she whispered.

"I'll never hurt you again, Heather. Not ever. Give me a second chance."

"You're asking a lot," she breathed.

"I know that." His forefinger traced the line of her upper lip. "I've smeared your lipstick."

She reached in her pocket for her kerchief and dabbed at her mouth as she walked along beside him toward the house. She glanced at him, noting his proud carriage, the arrogance of his straight nose, his glittering eyes. She never tired of looking at him.

The days went by pleasantly. Cole didn't make another move toward her, but they talked as they rarely had in the past. He took her riding early every morning, and once they reined in at the river where the fog was just rising off the water.

Cole dismounted, lifting her out of the saddle, and they stood together under a big-rooted oak tree at the water's edge.

"It's so peaceful here," Heather whispered, not wanting to disturb the almost primeval silence. "As if we're the only two people left in the world."

"Would it do me any good if we were?" he asked musingly, staring out across the fog-shrouded river to the dim trees beyond.

"What?" she asked, only half hearing him.

He leaned back against the huge trunk of the tree and tossed his wide-brimmed hat down beside it on the ground to study her. "Short hair and all," he murmured, "you're still the most beautiful woman I've ever seen. All light and color."

"That's only the outside, Cole," she reminded him. "How I look isn't what I am."

"I meant it as a compliment."

"Oh."

"Come here, honey." He caught her hand and pulled her in front of him, but she turned away. Holding her gently by the shoulders, he drew her back to him, his fingers tightening when she flinched. "Don't," he ground out, and there was anguish in his voice. "For God's sake, don't. I won't hurt you."

She closed her eyes, only to open them again with a weary sigh. She let her body relax against the hard strength of his while she watched the ripples in the fog-shrouded river.

"I'm not used to being touched," she said quietly. She hadn't meant to let that out, but the words slipped past her tight lips.

His hands loosened a little, but they remained on her upper arms, warm and comforting in the early-morning chill.

"I'm not used to it myself anymore," he admitted. His chest rose and fell heavily at her back. "It seems like years since we last stood here. You were about thirteen, weren't you, that day I took you and your friends down the river in a canoe?"

"And I fell out," she recalled with a laugh. "I was the wettest, most bedraggled thing. And you dragged me onto the bank, cursing a blue streak, your eyes blazing fire at me. . . . Gosh, you were scary, Cole."

"Scared, too," he chuckled. "I thought I'd lost you for sure. . . . Heather," he began on a more serious note, "I don't want you to be frightened of me ever again. Can't we go back to that night on the beach in Nassau, when you came into my arms without fear, as if you belonged there?''

She felt a tremor go through her at the words that brought back such aching memories. Her eyes closed involuntarily. "I don't want to remember that night," she said bitterly.

"Why?" he asked. "It was beautiful, Heather."

"You know why. Because it all meant nothing to you. I don't want to talk about it!" She tugged against his hands. "Oh, let me go, Cole!"

"I can't." He turned her and pulled her roughly into his arms. "My whole life seems to have gone up in smoke since we went to the Bahamas, do you know that? I've lost everything I ever cared about, and there doesn't seem to be chance in hell of getting anything back."

"You've got Tessa," she said, her voice muffled by the soft cotton front of his shirt.

"I haven't got her and I don't want her," he said tightly. "I threw her off the property the day before I came to find you, and I promised her if she ever set foot on Big Spur again, she'd regret it!"

She froze against him. "Cole!"

His face was like stone when she drew slightly away to look up at him. "Why?" she asked.

"I can't tell you." His hands moved up to tangle in her soft, wispy curls. "Woman, I've been so lonely without you."

"You had Big Spur," she reminded him, trying to keep her voice light.

"Cold comfort," he muttered. He traced the soft line of her mouth with a fingertip while the river gurgled and splashed along the banks. Above them, the leaves were rustling in the early morning breeze and the sun was just beginning to beat down on the water. "Can you forget the past if I ask you to?" he murmured gently. "Can you forgive the things I've said and let me get close to you again?"

"I've changed . . ." she began.

"We've both changed," he corrected. His eyes searched hers. "We'll go slow. We'll have to. But I want to get to know you again. And God knows, staying here a few weeks will give you a badly needed break." His lips compressed. "Or can't you live without your big time journalist that long?"

She wasn't going to tell him that she had never loved Gil Austin. She couldn't bear for him to know. "I can live without him," she said. Cole looked older, weary. Involuntarily, her fingers went up to touch the hollows under his silver eyes. "You look so tired," she murmured.

He caught her hand and pressed its soft palm to his lips. "I haven't been sleeping well," he said noncommittally. "Stay with me."

The way he phrased it made her pulse leap unexpectedly. She had felt numb inside for so long that it was a shock to find she had any emotions left in her. "I'll stay . . . for a week or so," she agreed finally.

His eyes dropped suddenly to her mouth. "Not on a strictly Platonic basis?" he murmured, bending his dark head.

She felt his warm breath on her mouth and her lips parted involuntarily. "Well..." she whispered uncertainly.

"Maybe...on a slightly Platonic basis?" he whispered, touching his mouth lightly to hers. "A few... very soft kisses?"

His words were drugging her. "A...a few kisses?" she murmured dazedly, her eyes on his parted lips.

"Um-hmm," he murmured, shifting so that he was leaning back against the tree with her slender body resting fully on his. He bent to brush his mouth against hers lazily. He lifted his head and studied her quietly, glancing past her at the river. "I've always loved this spot," he said absently. "Especially early in the morning like this, with the mist rising from the water."

She stared up at him, only half hearing the words, her eyes on his firm mouth, wanting it against hers just one more time.

He glanced down and saw the look on her face, and a strange, tender smile touched his chiseled lips. "Comfortable?" he murmured deeply, studying the way she was half-lying against him.

"You're very warm," she whispered.

"Honey, you don't know the half of it." He bent, and she waited for his mouth with a hunger she hadn't felt since that night in Nassau. Her eyes looked directly into his as their mouths met, touched, clung.

He drew back. "You like it like this, don't you?" he murmured softly. "Slow and gentle."

She tried to steady her breathing without success. "You don't like it," she whispered.

"I like it any way at all with you," he replied quietly.

She smiled at him, letting the barriers down for an instant.

"Smile at me like that, and I'd kill for you," he muttered, bending again, his mouth slower this time, the pressure slightly rougher, deeper. "It's been a long time since I've kissed you," he whispered against her lips. "I thought I'd never be able to again...."

She opened her eyes and looked at him. "Why, Cole?" she asked drowsily.

He didn't reply, but his face seemed to harden. "It doesn't matter. Come here."

He drew her closer, feeling her soft body yield to him without a struggle. His arms tightened, until he could feel every delicious inch of her against his powerful body, and he kissed her as if he never meant to stop.

She could feel the hunger in him, and it was almost as great as her own. It had been so long, so very long, and for a minute she forgot that she didn't trust him, didn't dare trust him, and she kissed him back with all her heart. With a sense of wonder she felt his long, hard body against hers, the warm biting pressure of his ardent mouth.

He felt her tremble and drew back, breathing hard, his eyes narrow on her flushed face. "You'll never feel this with another man," he said in a voice that was husky with emotion, "any more than I'll ever feel it with another woman. But you'd cut off your nose before you'd admit it, wouldn't you, Sunflower?"

She stared at him helplessly, hating her own weakness. There was a moment of quiet, broken only by the gurgling sound of the rushing river and the birds welcoming the rising sun. "I just don't know if I can trust you," she whispered softly, biting her lower lip.

She saw the pain in his eyes before he buried his face in her soft throat. His arms, trembling slightly, crushed her to him. "Heather," he breathed. He made of her name a prayer, a sweet sound that ached with longing. "Don't you think I'd take back the past few months if there was any human way to do it? Oh, my God, there were nights when I thought I'd go crazy, when I remembered the touch of you, the sound of your voice laughing.... I've gone to the stable in the middle of the night to saddle a horse and ride. But no matter how far I went, or how late I stayed awake, or how hard I worked, the memory of you stayed with me."

"You sent me away," she reminded him gently. The memory of that terrible day lingered in her sad, pale eyes, as she pushed against his chest. "Let me go, please," she said in a strained tone.

His hands held her for an instant before he reluctantly let her go. His eyes followed her as she went to stand by the riverbank and stooped to pick up some smooth, flat rocks. "So you don't trust me," he said flatly after a minute.

She caught the faint scent of smoke and knew he'd lit a cigarette even before he came to stand beside her and she saw it in his lean fingers. "I can't help it," she murmured. She tossed a stone into the river and glanced at his sharp, stern profile. "Cole, why won't you tell me what happened?"

He shifted, flexing his broad shoulders with a heavy sigh before he lifted the cigarette to his chiseled lips and took a long draw from it. "It was just something I found out that . . . made me believe there was no future for us."

She turned to study him, her eyes curious. "Did you really find something out?" she asked wistfully. "Or was it just that you didn't like the idea of being tied to anyone? You're a private person, Cole, freedom is like a religion to you. You don't want to give it up."

He met her eyes and one corner of his mouth went up. "There are worse things than losing it," he said quietly.

Her eyebrows arched. "Are you really Cole Everett, or an impostor taking his place?"

He looked down at her. "Do I kiss like an impostor?"

She smiled and lowered her eyes to his broad chest. "Talk about loaded questions," she murmured demurely.

He chuckled softly. "God, you've changed. Where's that little girl I used to tease?"

She peeked up at him through her lashes. "In some nightclub hiding under the piano, I think. Success is a quick road to maturity, my friend," she told him. "I feel absolutely ancient sometimes."

"You don't look it." His eyes boldly slid down her body, lingering on the soft curves of it. "You incredibly sexy creature," he murmured.

"Takes one to know one," she threw back, flirting with him and loving it. She enjoyed being his equal, having him treat her like an adult instead of a helpless, mindless child.

"That kind of talk will get you in trouble," he warned.

"What kind of trouble?" she asked with a wide smile.

He ground the cigarette out under his heel and started toward her. "Let me show you."

She laughed and dodged him, running back to the horses. He was right behind her, but she managed to vault into the saddle before he caught up.

"Coward," he murmured with a grin.

She laughed down at him. "You bet. I know all about you he-men who take women off into the woods."

He chuckled. "Why don't you come down off the horse and we'll discuss it?"

"I prefer to remain 'above it all,'" she replied, tongue-in-cheek.

He looked up at her with sparkling silver eyes, so handsome she wanted to climb down into his arms and succumb to the desire they were both feeling. But she wanted to be sure this time before she committed herself, before she trusted him again. She turned the horse with a wry glance in his direction and waited for him to mount and catch up before they left the river behind. Already, the mist was gone, and the sun had warmed the banks.

Chapter Eleven

If trusting Cole was difficult, getting along with him wasn't. Although she walked an emotional tightrope, he was the best of companions. He talked about his plans for Big Spur, his dreams, and she listened, interested. They went for long walks, they lingered over breakfast.

He was driving her around the feedlot when the rain began, and he turned the truck back toward home.

"So much for that," he chuckled. "We'll mire up to the axles if we don't get back on the gravel."

He drove until they reached the graveled stretch of farm road, but at that instant the rain began coming down in buckets. Cole pulled the truck over to the side of the road and cut off the engine, easing it into park before he took his foot off the brake.

The cab of the truck seemed as intimate as a bedroom with the blanket of rain protecting them from prying eyes. And Cole, with his hair rumpled, his denim shirt straining across the powerful muscles of his chest, and his jeans clinging to the hard lines of his thighs, was so attractive she couldn't drag her eyes away from him. Her heart came into her throat. She tore her eyes away from his suddenly piercing gaze and looked out the window at the long stretch of land, barely visible in the driving rain. "Lucky old corn," she murmured lightly. "I'll bet it's been praying for rain."

"So have my cattle," he returned. He pulled a cigarette out of his pocket, glanced her way, and suddenly repocketed it. "I'll wait until I can open a window," he murmured. "You're still a little hoarse from the pneumonia."

"You're very considerate," she teased.

"I haven't always been." He turned sideways to study her while the rain beat an erratic rhythm against the metal roof. His eyes glittered possessively over her slender body. In her pink sundress, with its brief bodice, she looked unusually lovely, the short haircut adding sophistication to her poise. "You're so beautiful," Cole murmured. He reached out and touched her mouth with a long, caressing forefinger. "Come here. I want to feel your mouth under mine."

Her heart turned over. She stared at him helplessly until he caught her waist and lifted her onto his lap. Her head fell back naturally on his shoulder as he kissed her. "Cole..." she murmured under his warm, rough lips.

"Shhh," he whispered. "We can't talk and kiss at the same time."

"But..."

"Don't you want to kiss me?" he whispered softly, nipping her lips tenderly.

She gave in all at once and let her body relax in his arms. "Yes," she admitted with a moan.

"Then show me," he invited, nudging her lips apart with his.

She reached up and wrapped her arms around him, returning the kiss as ardently as he gave it, feeling the slightly rough texture of his face against hers.

"Here," he whispered, pressing her fingers to the buttons of his shirt and then leaning back to watch her fumble with the buttonholes until she had it open.

He guided her fingers against the hard muscles of his chest, his stomach, watching her face the whole time, as if the emotions chasing across it fascinated him. "Mmm," he murmured, his pleasure in the caress obvious.

"Just don't... rush me," she whispered.

"When have I ever done that?" he asked quietly. He ran his hand from her cheek to her collarbone, then down over the soft fabric covering her high breasts. "No, don't try to stop me," he said softly, ignoring the fingers that attempted to dislodge his invading hand. "I want to touch you as much as you want to touch me, and there's no sane reason why I shouldn't. You belong to me. You can deny it until hell freezes over, but every time I touch you, your body welcomes me, and you know it."

"You're going too fast," she whispered achingly, twisting under the expert pressure of his fingers as they moved against her soft curves.

"No, honey, I'm not," he whispered back. His lips pressed tenderly against her forehead. "We haven't made love in a long time, and I'm hungry for you. If you'd admit it, you're just as hungry for me. Do you remember that night on the beach, Heather, when I laid you down in the sand and touched you the first time? Do you remember how you moaned and arched toward me?"

"Cole, don't..." she pleaded, hating the memory even as the magic came sweeping back at the mention of it.

"I want to," he whispered against her mouth. "I need to. My God, I've missed you!"

He drew her up against him and kissed her roughly, the hunger in him so evident that it almost frightened her. All her hard-won poise and sophistication slipped away as she began to realize that he was in earnest now. This was no flirtatious game that she could stop when she chose. He wasn't playing, not now.

"Cole..." she whispered, weakening, her fingers slowly caressing his bronzed chest.

"I want you," he whispered, the words soft and slow. "I want to touch you, to feel you tremble under my hands. I want to hear those sweet little sounds you make when I love you...."

Love. Love. She remembered telling him she loved him, and his cool, painful rejection of her. Without thinking, she drew back, the wariness in her eyes again, the memory falling between them like a curtain.

"Stop looking back," he said quietly. His breath was coming hard and heavy, and he looked alarmingly masculine, sensual, with his dark hair and blazing silver eyes. He was so close she could feel every hard muscle of his torso against her softness.

"I can't help it," she whispered.

"I know," he ground out. "Oh, God, I'd give anything to be able to take back the things I said. You can't know how it hurt me to say them."

"Why, Cole?" she asked, drawing away to look straight into his glittering eyes. "Tell me why!"

"I can't. My sweet baby, I'd only hurt you more, don't you see?" He sighed deeply, tracing her mouth with a slow, caressing finger. "It's better forgotten. Perhaps, in time, you'll be able to forgive me."

"I can do that easily enough," she admitted. "But it's hard to...to trust you. It's almost impossible."

"I won't push you away again," he told her, his face solemn, his eyes darkening with emotion. "No matter what happens, I'll never walk away from you. If anyone turns away this time, Heather, it will be you."

She searched his eyes quietly. "Would you care?"

His eyes closed briefly. "Yes," he ground out. His eyes opened, stormy, like rain clouds. "Yes, I'd care. Can't you tell? Can't you feel it when I hold you?"

"That's...desire," she corrected, dropping her eyes to the hard, quick pulse at his throat.

"Is that all it is?"

She shrugged. "I don't know."

He tilted her head back so that he could see her face. "You always hold back with me. When we talk. When we make love. It was like that long before I made you leave me. Why, Heather? What makes you so afraid to give in to me?"

"I don't want to lose myself in you," she admitted, letting the words slip past her tight lips.

"Are you afraid you might?" he growled. He eased her down against him, her head cradled in the crook of his arm as he bent over her. "Why don't you give in to it, just once, and see what it can be like?"

She felt something unutterably primitive stir deep inside her slender body as he kissed her, his mouth possessive, demanding. His arms crushed her nearer while the rain continued to beat down on the metal roof of the cab, shutting them away from the world. She felt suddenly reckless, all woman. Why should Cole have all the magic? She reached up to hold him tightly, her mouth answering his, her teeth nipping at his hungry lips, her tongue tempting him, a strange half-moan coming from somewhere deep in her throat.

He drew back, the hunger he was feeling showing in every hard line of his face.

"Don't hold back this time," he ground out. "Show me how much you've changed."

Her nails pressed against the nape of his neck and her eyes slitted as they gazed, smoldering, into his. "It might surprise you," she murmured, drawing his head down to her parted lips. She kissed him hungrily, letting all the lonely nights, all the empty days, pour into that warm, close embrace as she told him without words that she'd ached for him.

He returned the kiss as hungrily as she gave it, but there was still a strange tenderness in his action, an intangible emotion that separated it from lust as surely as water divides land.

The sound of another vehicle brought his head up, stilled the deft hands that had slid under the straps of her bodice to trace patterns on the skin of her bare back while they kissed as if they never meant to stop. "Oh, hell," he ground out, recognizing one of the ranch trucks. Clearing the foggy window with his sleeve, he was able to make out Danny at the wheel.

"Did we do that?" Heather murmured, sitting up to stare half-amused at the fog.

He glanced at her, his mouth sensuous, his hair mussed, his whole look possessive. "Sexy little thing, aren't you?" he murmured.

One silky eyebrow went up. "I had a good teacher," she replied.

Danny had stopped his truck beside Cole's and now he rolled down the window, waiting for Cole to do the same.

"There's some flooding down on the Youngman bottoms," Danny called. "The boys are moving the cattle now, but it's touch and go. Jack sent me for the big trailer."

"I'll give you a hand. Meet me at the barn." He rolled the window back up and started the truck with a wistful glance at Heather's mouth. "Damned cattle," he murmured as he pulled back out into the road and followed Danny toward the ranch.

"That's the first time I've ever heard you say that." She laughed softly.

"Damned cowboys, too," he said with a short laugh. "When Danny tells them about these windows, I'll have hell to pay."

She flushed a little. "Embarrassed, Mr. Everett?" she teased.

He glared at her. "I'm too old to make love to women in parked cars."

"It's a truck," she pointed out.

"Don't confuse the issue with a lot of facts." He chuckled. He eyed her lazily across the seat. "Come here, you delicious little morsel."

She responded mindlessly to the sensual note in his voice, sliding across the seat to him. His arm looped around her shoulders and pulled her closer so that she could feel the powerful muscles in the thigh that pressed against her leg.

He eased down on the brake and bent to kiss her warmly, lazily, tasting her mouth with evident enjoyment.

She drew away from the warm, moist pressure of his lips. "You'll wreck the truck," she murmured.

"I've never wished harder for a flat tire," he said, dropping another kiss on her lips before he turned his attention back to the road. "God, I love kissing you!"

She nestled closer, resting her cheek against his soft cotton shirt. "I love it, too," she whispered, all the strength gone out of her.

"I hope you've got an evening gown here," he remarked.

"Yes, I have. Why?"

"We're going dancing tonight, flood or no flood."

She smiled up at him. "I can't think of anything I'd like more."

He lifted a mischievous eyebrow. "I can," he murmured suggestively.

"Lecher," she accused.

"Puritan," he threw back. "Wear something strapless."

"Why?" she asked without thinking, and that eyebrow went up again. He laughed at the scarlet blush on her face.

He pulled up in front of the door. "Be ready by six."

"Will you be back from the swamp by then?" she asked.

He tugged at a short lock of her hair. "I'd be back from hell by then if it meant spending the evening with you. Get out of here before I yield to temptation."

She laughed delightedly, pausing to press a quick kiss against his mouth before she jerked open the door.

He stared after her, half-shocked at the gesture. "You kiss *me* all the time lately," she said saucily.

"Yes," he admitted, "but I think that's the first time you've kissed me."

Her eyes were sad for a moment. "You didn't want me to before."

His eyes searched hers quietly. "Honey, you'd laugh if you knew the truth." He put the truck in gear. "Six, woman!"

"Yes, sir!" she called back, laughing as she hadn't in months. Suddenly all the barriers were coming down, and she could love Cole again, even if he only wanted her. She'd make the most of what little time she had with him. For the present, just being with him was enough.

It was exciting to go out with Cole, and she watched the glances he attracted from other women with a slightly jealous eye. In her long white gown with its simple lines and revealing side slit, she was attracting her own share of attention, but she hardly noticed, so absorbed was she in Cole.

He hadn't taken his eyes off her since they'd left the house, and now he was staring pointedly at the strapless bodice of her dress. "Took me seriously, did you?" he asked as they lingered over coffee after a meal of steak and lobster followed by cherries jubilee.

She averted her eyes. She felt as though her heart would burst at the sight of him, he was so ruggedly handsome in his dark evening clothes. "As it happens, it was the only gown in my closet," she replied truthfully, reluctant to admit that she'd almost switched it for an elegant pantsuit.

He cupped his hands around the coffee cup, his eyes narrowing on her flushed face. "I like the feel of your skin," he murmured. "Like silk, with a warmth and perfume all its own."

"Stop it," she whispered frantically.

He chuckled softly. "I thought you were all grown up."

"I feel about thirteen when you say things like that. It's like shooting fish in a barrel," she accused, "and you should be ashamed."

"I'm not." His eyes dropped to her bodice again. "I even remember the taste of you...."

"Let's dance!" she said quickly.

He got to his feet and held out his hand to lead her onto the dance floor. She stood stiffly in his arms while they moved around the room, dodging other couples.

"Are you afraid to come any closer?" he murmured, a look of amusement in his glittering eyes.

She looked up at him through her impossibly long lashes. "I'm afraid, period," she admitted shakily. "Cole, what are you trying to do to me?"

"Prove to you that what was between us hasn't vanished," he replied, all the teasing gone as he looked at her. "I want to make love to you. I want to kiss you until you stop being afraid and let go, the way you did in the truck this afternoon."

"In other words," she managed, trying to be adult about it, "you want to sleep with me."

"Honey, what I want doesn't have a damned thing to do with sleep," he said flatly. "No, don't hide your eyes, look at me."

She didn't want to, but that commanding tone didn't give her a choice. His face was unusually solemn.

"It's good having you home again," he murmured. "It gives me an excuse not to work myself sick."

She smiled up at him. "You've needed an excuse for years," she told him. "I still remember all the weekends Emma and I spent by ourselves because you were away on business—I almost never saw you when I was home from school on holidays. You've done little else but work for Big Spur."

"Big Spur is more than a ranch now," he reminded her. "It's a corporation. During the past few years, it's been growing so fast I hardly have time to breathe."

"You're breathing now," she murmured, watching his chest. She slid her hands down from his neck to move them caressingly against the softness of his shirt. "Very fast, too," she whispered. She deliberately moved close so that she could feel his powerful legs against hers.

With a harsh mutter, he caught her waist and put her away from him, none too gently. His eyes blazed into hers, and it was like going back in time to that night in his study when she'd confessed everything she felt for him, and he'd pushed her away and said, "I'm sorry, I can't love you that way."

Her mind whirled with the words, and it was all there in her eyes, the rejection, the hurt, the humiliation.

He read that look on her face, but understanding came too late. "Heather..." he began.

She moved back when he reached out for her, like a small wounded thing trying to escape the hunter. "Can we go home?" she asked gently, forcing a smile to her mouth. "It's getting late and I'm...I'm very tired...." Her voice broke on the word, and she turned and almost ran for the ladies' room.

There was another woman in it who glanced at the newcomer's unhappy face, then smiled gently and left Heather alone. The minute the door swung shut, she collapsed in tears, feeling as if her heart would break in two. Cole was beyond all understanding. It was just as she'd feared. This was all some monstrous game he was playing. She didn't know if she could bear to go out that door again, to face him after this newest rejection. Blow hot, blow cold, she thought, and laughed hysterically for a minute before she brought herself back under control.

She'd have to leave the ranch. She knew that now. There was no way she could stay and maintain her sanity. She washed her face and dried it with a paper towel, pausing just long enough to repair some of the damage to her makeup. Hiding in here wouldn't solve anything, she'd have to go home with him or walk, and it was a long way on foot.

A well-dressed woman, obviously an employee of the restaurant, poked her head in the door and smiled at Heather. "Is your name Heather?" she asked.

Heather nodded, the ravages of tears plainly visible on her face.

"Well, there's a very good-looking man out there who just offered to go down on his knees to you if you'll come out," she announced with a giggle. "I'd take him up on it myself; he's a dish!"

Tears sprang up again in Heather's soft blue eyes, but the picture of Cole on his elegant knees was enough to bring a smile to her lips as well. She followed the woman out into the cozy lounge where Cole was standing with the brim of his dress Stetson clenched in one lean hand.

"Let's go home," he said gently. "I've got to talk to you."

"All right, Cole," she agreed, but she didn't look him in the eyes.

* * *

She got out of the car after their silent ride home and rushed up the steps, fumbling for her house key. She didn't really want any postmortems, she only wanted her bed, and if she hurried, she'd have time to escape while Cole was putting the car in the garage.

She hadn't counted on Cole entering the house right behind her. She'd no sooner opened the door and walked into the dimly lit hall than he closed the door again and got between Heather and the staircase.

"Not yet," he said firmly. "First we talk."

"I'm tired, Cole," she murmured.

"My God, so am I. Tired of pretense and misunderstandings and a past that's tearing my soul to pieces," he ground out. He sighed heavily. "Talk to me. Don't run away."

"What is there to talk about?" she managed weakly, avoiding his eyes. "First you kiss me, then you send me away and tell me you can't love me. Then you say hateful things to me, and bring me back...and you won't tell me why!"

He sucked in a harsh breath and rammed his hands into his pockets. "No one likes to admit being stupid," he growled. "Least of all, me. I made one hell of a mistake. I listened to the wrong person, and tried to protect you from something that didn't exist. I don't want to go into it. It's too involved, and I've told you a dozen times already, it's unnecessary. Forget the past, will you?"

"I can't!" Her eyes gleamed with tears. "I can't. You're cold and hot, and I don't know how you expect me to trust you...."

"If you cared enough, you would," he shot at her, his eyes fiery.

"After the way you've treated me?!"

His eyes closed. "I keep hoping for miracles, I suppose," he said after a minute, searching her wan face. "And after tonight we'll go back to square one, won't we?"

"No, we won't. I'm going back to Houston tomorrow," she told him, surprised at the sudden paleness of his face. "I've had all I can take, Cole. I can't stay here any longer."

"Because of tonight?" he asked curtly.

She turned away. "I'm going to bed."

"Like hell you are!"

Before she had time to move or react, he swung her up into his steely arms and headed straight for the den, his grip unbreakable, his face hard, implacable. He shouldered his way into the room where a single lamp was burning and kicked the door shut behind him.

"Cole, what are you doing?" she got out.

"You've made up your mind. Nothing I do is going to change it, so I might as well be hanged for a sheep as a lamb, isn't that how the saying goes?" He tossed her down onto the burgundy leather couch and paused just long enough to shed his jacket, rip off his tie, and open the neck of his shirt before he came down beside her.

She was too shocked to even fight him. Her eyes looked straight into his as he let the full weight of his powerful body ease down onto hers, pressing it deeper into the padding of the sofa.

"You're . . . heavy," she whispered unsteadily. She was suddenly aware of his spicy cologne, the clean scent of his hard-muscled body, the smoky warmth of his breath on her lips.

His fingers tangled in her short hair and held her head where he wanted it. "You won't notice that in a minute," he ground out, bending to crush her mouth for an instant under the warm, moist pressure of his. "When I get through with you, you won't even remember it. By God, you'll feel as if you're committing sacrilege when you let another man touch you . . . !"

His mouth crushed hers again, hard this time, rough, as if he didn't care that he hurt her, his fingers tugging painfully at her hair.

"Cole, you're hurting me," she whispered shakily against his mouth.

He hesitated long enough to look down into her eyes, and all of a sudden his fingers relaxed, became caressing, and some of the wildness seemed to go out of him. "I want you so, Heather," he said quietly, deep velvet in his voice. "Feel this," he whispered, opening his shirt to take her small hand and slide it under the warm silk. "Do you feel how my body trembles when you touch me? How my heart pounds? Sweet love, you don't know how I ache."

She stared at him, feeling that hard, heavy beat under her fingers, the faint tremor in his powerful arms.

"God, Heather, why do you think I pushed you away?" he ground out, bending, his mouth poised a fraction of an inch above hers. "If I hadn't, I'd have kissed you right there in front of the whole damned crowd. I couldn't have helped myself... and you thought I was rejecting you, didn't you? As if I could," he whispered half angrily just before his mouth ground into hers.

She felt the hunger in him, like a fever that burned them both. Her slender body relaxed just a little under the long hard pressure of his, and she gave in to her desire gracefully, loving him so deeply that nothing he did would be unwelcome.

Her fingers opened the rest of the buttons on his shirt and slid over the hard muscles of his chest, into the thick hair that arrowed down his muscular body past his leather belt. She felt his hands guiding, his softly whispered words making music in her mind as he taught her all the sweet lessons of loving. The silence was barely broken by the sound of the grandfather clock in the hall and the rasp of Cole's breathing.

He moved then, settling her back on the sofa, his long, powerful body covering hers completely. She felt his full weight with a sense of absolute awe, her eyes staring straight into his as she felt his hands sliding under her to undo the zipper that held her dress in place. "No, don't stop me," he whispered gently, easing the fabric away. Gently, he moved against her until they melted together from the waist up in a slow, sensual rhythm. "This is part of loving."

She felt his mouth touch hers and her short, sharp nails bit into his shoulders as the contact with his warm, hair-roughened chest made her feel an almost primitive abandon. She loved him so, it was all she could do not to give in completely, but she couldn't, she couldn't! Her eyes were tortured as she tried to ease her mouth away from his.

"Don't do that," he whispered hungrily. "Open your mouth to mine, Heather. Come on, honey, give me your mouth...." He found it and took it, cherishing it in a hungry silence that made nonsense of her struggles. She moaned, moving sensually under his formidable weight, her mind going mad at the sensations he was causing.

"Sweet love," he whispered against her mouth, feeling the passion begin to stir in the soft body under his. Her arms slid around him and her mouth became suddenly eager, hungry, asking now instead of shrinking away, answering his ardor with an innocent hunger that tested his control to its limits.

She moved unconsciously, and he groaned against her mouth. She stared into his eyes, shocked.

"Don't do that again," he whispered gruffly. "You'll drive me right over the edge. Or was that what you had in mind? Do you want to lie in my arms tonight and let me make a woman of you?"

The flush spread all over her cheeks, down her throat. "I...I..." she stammered.

"I'll be exquisitely gentle with you," he whispered against her soft mouth, his voice beguiling, his lips tender, coaxing. His hands ran down her smooth body, touching, exploring, and she moaned at the expert sureness of them, unconsciously arching toward him. "Come to bed with me."

Her body trembled wildly and even as she realized how desperately she wanted it, she was pulling away from him to press her hot face into the soft throw cushions. "No!" she whispered tearfully. "Oh, God, no, I can't!"

He froze beside her, as if he'd stopped breathing. A minute later, she felt his weight shift as he got to his feet. She heard him move away, light a cigarette. He muttered something as he went to stand by the darkened window. "Was I too intimate with you?" he asked curtly. "My God, I've been walking on eggshells. I thought I was going slowly enough even for your prim little mind."

She flared up, not realizing that he was speaking out of frustration, not anger. "What do you want?" she asked through tight lips, her back ramrod straight as she sat up on the sofa and stared at him.

He turned, one hand in his pocket, his eyes blazing in his dark face. "What do you think I want?"

"Me, I suppose," she murmured.

"Damned straight. You. In my bed, all night, every night, starting now."

She hated the heat in her cheeks, the whip in Cole's voice. She glared at him. "Not without love," she ground out. "Not without love, Cole."

He went white. Absolutely white, and something like pain was visible in his eyes before he turned his back on her. And she knew then that it was true—he didn't love her. Couldn't, wouldn't love her.

"I'm going back to Houston tomorrow afternoon," she said quietly. "I think that will be better for both of us, in the long run."

All the ferocity seemed to drain out of him then. "Perhaps you're right. If you still can't trust me..."

"How can you ask me to, when you won't explain anything, Cole?" she asked miserably. "What guarantee have I got that you won't reject me all over again?"

"Because, damn it, I'm telling you so!" he shot back.

"That isn't enough."

He drew in a deep, slow breath. "Then go back to Houston."

She got to her feet, staring at his rigid back. He stood like a statue, unmoving. "Cole..."

"I've got cattle coming in tomorrow," he said in a hatefully casual tone. "I'll be out at the holding pens if you care to say good-bye."

His careless tone hurt more than his temper. She went to the door in a fog, her heart leaden, her eyes stinging with unshed tears. "I've already said it," she said tightly. She went out the door without looking back and closed it firmly behind her.

She barely slept. The next morning, she wanted nothing more than to apologize, but Cole had already gone out by the time she got to the breakfast table.

"Good thing, too," Mrs. Jones grumbled. She was working in the kitchen while Heather helped with the dishes. "He nearly bit my head off when I asked him if he wanted me to set him a place for lunch. He's in an awful temper."

Heather didn't say a word. But tears misted her eyes while she dried the sparkling clean dishes and half-heartedly listened to Mrs. Jones talk about a new recipe she was going to try. She didn't want to go back to Houston, she didn't want to leave Cole. But she had to get away while she still could. It would have to be today.

She wouldn't see Cole before she left. That hurt, too, but there was no way around it. He was furious, so he'd stay out all day giving his men hell the way he usually did when he was working something out of his system. He wouldn't be home before dark, and she would be gone by then.

She was so wound up in her problems, she didn't even hear the knock at the door until Mrs. Jones went to answer it. There were voices in the hall, Mrs. Jones' and one Heather could hardly believe she was hearing: Tessa!

She tossed down the dishrag and went into the hall.

"Mr. Cole will skin you alive if he catches you here," Mrs. Jones was telling the white-faced brunette.

"I know," she said shortly, glaring at Heather. "He'd do anything to keep Heather from learning the truth, but I'm going to tell her."

Heather gaped at her. "The truth about what?"

Tessa glanced at Mrs. Jones. "Not here. Come on." She led the way into the living room as if it was her house, leaving Heather to follow.

"Well?" Heather asked, slamming the door behind them. She positively glared at Tessa, her blue eyes flashing.

Tessa was wary of the new Heather, the one she'd discovered that night in the dressing room at the Golden Gun. There was a fire in the younger woman's eyes, and Tessa sensed its strength. "It's something you're entitled to know," she muttered.

Heather sat down comfortably in an armchair and stared at her. "Well?" she repeated.

Tessa sat down, too, on the edge of the sofa, her hands moving nervously in her lap. "It's a long story," she said.

"Then you'd better get started," Heather replied.

Tessa shifted uncomfortably. "It...it all started when your mother had...when Big Jace came over one night while your father was away...."

"And seduced my mother?" Heather asked with a faintly amused smile.

Tessa blinked at her. "What?"

"You aren't by any chance going to suggest that Big Jace was my father as well as Cole's?" Heather asked politely.

"But, he was . . . !"

Heather sighed. "Tessa, I don't suppose you're capable of really loving anyone, but maybe you can understand if I put it like this. Big Jace worshiped Emma. He'd gladly have died for her. Men who care that much about any one woman aren't going to risk everything just for a few hours with some frigid iceberg like my mother."

Tessa couldn't believe her ears. She stared at Heather with wide, shocked eyes.

"Didn't you know? My parents had separate bedrooms. Big Jace couldn't have seduced my mother without a blowtorch, because she was pure ice from the neck down. She liked to flirt with men, to get them hungry . . . but she never had any real love to give. I know, I lived with her all those empty years before Emma came into this house. And I know better than most how deeply Emma and Big Jace loved each other. So don't come over here telling me fairy tales. And I wouldn't take that tale to Cole either, if I were you, he'd very likely . . ." She stopped in mid-sentence, staring at the flush that covered Tessa's face. All of a sudden, everything made sense. Everything!

"You told him that in Nassau," Heather breathed. "You told him Big Jace was my father, and he believed you!"

Tessa's lower lip trembled. She glared at the younger woman. "Cole is mine! He's mine, I've waited years for him, I've loved him! He belongs to me! I'm not going to let you have him!"

"You love him?" Heather scoffed, her eyes blazing. "If you cared even a tiny bit, you'd want him to be happy. You're selfish, Tessa, you only think about what you want. If Cole cared about you, he wouldn't have to be blackmailed to leave me alone. He'd...he'd hang around you like a chain at your neck, he'd hardly be able to keep his hands off you." She heard her own words and realized with a start that was exactly how Cole had been acting with her. Could he care? Could he!

"He'd love me if it weren't for you!" Tessa cried, jumping to her feet, her huge dark eyes brimming with tears. "He believed me when I told him about Deidre and Big Jace! He'd still believe it if Emma hadn't left him that letter!"

"I feel sorry for you," Heather said quietly.

"Don't waste your pity!" She whirled and went to the door. Her eyes flashed accusingly at Heather. "You're nothing like your mother," she stated contemptuously.

"No, I'm not," Heather agreed with a smile.

Tessa slammed out the door. Heather ran upstairs to put on her boots, the light of dawning happiness in her face.

* * *

It was one of those rare times when nothing seems impossible. Heather leaned over the mare's mane, giving her her head. Her eyes were full of hope, her short hair flying wildly around her flushed face.

She understood Cole now as she never had before. It had been because of what Tessa told him that he'd sent her away. It had been out of love, out of a misguided attempt to spare her from further heartache. And his pride, that deep-rooted masculine pride that was as much a part of him as his silver eyes, had kept him from admitting how easily he'd taken Tessa's word for gospel. But it would be all right now. Everything would be all right. She clung to the horse's mane and dug her heels in.

It took some searching to find Cole, who'd left the holding pens and was out helping some of his men look for a few strays that had gotten loose in the thicket by the river.

The men were taking time out for a cup of coffee, sitting idly around a small camp fire, some talking, one whittling. Cole sat on a log, all alone, his hands around a metal cup, staring into space. He looked so lonely. Heather's heart gave a lurch at the sight of him.

She reined in and swung down out of the saddle gracefully, aware of Cole's start of surprise as he spotted her and stood up. She smiled at the men as she walked into the small camp, but the smile faded when her questioning eyes met Cole's.

"Well?" he asked.

Her nerve almost deserted her. "I, uh, I…can I talk to you for a minute?" she managed finally.

He set down his cup without another word. "Ten more minutes, Bob," he told one of the men, who nodded and murmured something before he went to take Cole's place on the log.

Cole walked beside her down a wooded path, stopping within sight of the other cowboys. She leaned back against the trunk of a large oak, shy with him in a way she hadn't been for a long time.

"Did you decide to say good-bye after all?" he asked coldly.

She stared at his handsome face, looking for the first time behind that icy facade and seeing the hurt that was responsible for it.

"In a way," she murmured, and she smiled at him. "Remember what you told me last night?"

Both eyebrows went up. "I told you a lot last night."

She peeked at him through her lashes. "You said you wanted to sleep with me."

He leaned a hand against a tree beside her head and stared at her curiously. "So I did."

"Well, I came to tell you that I've changed my mind."

His hand slipped and he caught himself just in time. His eyes blazed down at her. "You what?"

"I'll sleep with you, if that's what you want." She reached out a finger and touched a button on his shirt, sliding her finger in between the opening to touch his bare chest.

"Heather..." he warned huskily.

"Your heart's beating very fast," she remarked. She parted her lips deliberately, smiling when his eyes followed the movement hungrily.

"Honey, you are tempting fate," he ground out.

"Well, it isn't for lack of effort, that's for sure," she told him. "What do I have to do to seduce you? Strip? It might embarrass the men, especially since I'm not wearing anything under this blouse...."

"Oh, my God," he bit off, and she could see his teeth clench. "You asked for it, damn you."

He caught her around the waist with a steely hand and slammed her body against his, bending to take her mouth with a goaded violence. She smiled under his furious lips, relaxing against him sensually, letting him ravish her mouth, glorying in his rough ardor.

The murmurs and conspiratorial laughter of the cowboys brought him back to his senses. He drew back and glared down at her, his breath uneven, a visible tremor in the hard-muscled arm holding her.

"Do you really have to work cattle right now?" she asked in a husky whisper.

"Hell, no," he said gruffly. "Danny, bring the jeep home when you finish," he called over his shoulder, dragging Heather along behind him by the hand.

"You bet, boss. Don't get lost!" Danny called.

"Where are we going?" Heather asked as they wound through the woods past tall pines and small fir trees, crunching over dead logs and through leafy bushes.

"Some place where the boys can't see us." He stopped in a clearing where pine needles were thick on the ground and turned, his eyes glittering, his face hard as stone. If he expected her to run, he was disappointed. She went to him like a homing pigeon, going on tiptoe to link her hands around his neck. Her eyes were unafraid, her body already yielding to the strength of his.

"I love you," she whispered softly, watching the shock register in his eyes with a feeling of joy. "I love you with all my heart, and I'll be anything and everything you want me to be. I'll sleep with you, I'll help you punch cattle, I'll sit and watch you do the books, I'll cook puddings for you when Mrs. Jones goes on vacation.... I'm not going back to Houston, Cole. All I want is right here. Everything I want in all the world is you."

His eyes searched hers in a silence broken only by the rustling leaves and the soft, pine-scented wind.

"I don't understand," he whispered shakily. "And right now, I don't care. Make me believe it, Heather. I've waited for this for months, wanting you, needing you, loving you...."

She felt his mouth on hers with a sense of wonder. She could barely believe what she'd just heard, hadn't it been something about loving?

She kissed him back hungrily, dimly aware that he was drawing her down to the ground, laying her gently back on the pine needles, his body heavy and warm against hers. His hands slid under the loose blouse, confirming the truth of her earlier statement. He ran his lean, hard fingers over her body with possession in his touch, watching her eyes while he explored every sweet, soft curve of her.

She smiled up at him, arching under his hands, her breath catching in her throat at the sensations he was causing.

"Do you like it?" he murmured, all arrogance now. Gone was the ruffled man she'd tried to seduce a few minutes earlier.

"Oh, yes, I like it," she whispered, lifting to meet his descending mouth. "Cole, I love you so!"

"I love you, too, honey," he murmured ardently. "God, I love you! But I still don't understand why you came out here with seduction on your mind."

She linked her hands behind his head, watching him flick open the buttons of her blouse.

"I'll catch cold," she warned him.

"No, you won't," he murmured with a wicked smile, laughing as she gasped under the sudden invasion of his mouth against her neck.

"Tessa came to see me," she whispered over his head.

"Did she?" He stiffened, but he didn't raise his eyes. "What did she tell you?"

"About Big Jace and my mother." She laughed. "Poor Tessa, she did give it a good try, didn't she?"

He lifted his head then, his eyes quiet, searching. "You didn't believe her."

She shook her head, sighing lazily. "Oh, Cole, didn't you really know how Big Jace worshiped Emma? She and I talked a lot about marriage before she died. She told me that if I ever found a love like she and your father shared, I'd be the luckiest woman alive. She knew Deidre had tried to seduce him; she even laughed about it. But she trusted Big Jace . . . the way I've learned to trust you." She studied Cole's beloved face with soft, worshiping eyes. "Emma always knew he wouldn't willingly do anything to hurt her."

"You're right, of course," he said in a tortured voice, and there was remorse in his eyes, his face. "Can you ever forgive me for the pain I caused you? I believed Tessa's lies, and I thought I had no choice but to drive you away from me."

"Out of love," she whispered. "You loved me enough to let me go, because you wanted what was best for me. And you're asking me for forgiveness?" Tears ran from her eyes. "Oh, Cole, forgive *me* for not trusting you. How it must have hurt you when I turned away. . . ."

He brushed the tears away with his lips, tender, soft, slow on her wan face. "Shhhh," he whispered. "Love me. We'll heal each other."

She welcomed his mouth, his caressing hands. "Here?" she whispered shakily.

He chuckled against her mouth, then left a trail of kisses down her bare body to the waistband of her slacks. "Are you shy of the squirrels?" he murmured, nipping her soft flesh with his teeth.

She smoothed back the dark, unruly hair over his forehead, her eyes soft with longing. "I'm shy of you," she corrected. "But that won't last long. I love you very much."

"I love you." He bent over her, his eyes darkening, tender. "No, darling, not here, not now. But soon. I want a ring on your finger before you run away again."

"I won't run from you again," she promised. She studied his face and smiled. "Can we have babies?"

"As many as you want." He grinned. "But how are you going to manage a career and motherhood as well?"

"The same way you'll manage to be a rancher and a father," she whispered softly.

He searched her eyes quietly, everything he felt for her there for her to see. "Not while the boys are young."

She smiled up at him with her eyes full of dreams. "Not while the boys are young, darling," she promised as she drew his mouth down to hers.

* * * * *